MY OWN GROUND

BOOKS BY HUGH NISSENSON

A Pile of Stones
Notes from the Frontier
In the Reign of Peace
My Own Ground

MY OWN GROUND

Hugh Nissenson

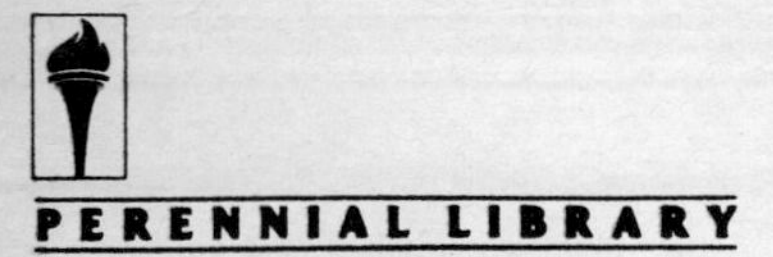

Harper & Row, Publishers
New York, Cambridge, Philadelphia, San Francisco
London, Mexico City, São Paulo, Singapore, Sydney

A hardcover edition of this book was published by Farrar, Straus & Giroux, Inc. It is here reprinted by arrangement with Farrar, Straus & Giroux, Inc.

 For information address Harper & Row, Publishers, Inc., 10 East 53rd Street, New York, N.Y. 10022. Published simultaneously in Canada by Fitzhenry & Whiteside Limited, Toronto.

First PERENNIAL LIBRARY edition published 1987.

Library of Congress Cataloging-in-Publication Data
Nissenson, Hugh.
My own ground.
I. Title.
[PS3564.I8M9 1987] 813'.54 86-45676
ISBN 0-06-097075-8 (pbk.)

---

87 88 89 90 91 MPC 10 9 8 7 6 5 4 3 2 1

For MARILYN, whose book this is;
and for KATE, whose book this will someday be.

I am grateful for assistance received during the writing of this book from the Creative Artists Public Service Program (CAPS).

H.N.

He was wise, he saw mysteries and knew secret things, he brought us a tale of the days before the flood. He went on a long journey, was weary, worn out with labor, and returning, engraved the whole story on a stone.

THE EPIC OF GILGAMESH

MY OWN GROUND

1

IN THE SUMMER OF 1912, when I was fifteen years old, Schlifka the pimp offered me ten bucks to tell him when Hannah Isaacs showed up on Orchard Street in the building where I lived.

"Take it or leave it," he said. "No questions asked."

"Ten bucks?"

"Just say the word."

"Yeah."

We shook on it. I got a whiff of his cigar. "I knew you was my man," he said. "I knew it the first time we met."

We'd met on a Wednesday night, the week before. He was on the stoop when I got home from work at seven. I recognized him by his red hair, parted in the middle, which was slicked down with brilliantine; it shone in the light from the gas jet behind him on the hallway wall. His black-patent-leather shoes were shiny, too; even the high heels. Come to think of it, I noticed them later: after supper, when I went back outside for a breath of air. He stared me down.

"You must be Jake Brody," he said. "The kid from the third floor that speaks English. I heard a lot about you."

"That makes us even."

"You speak real good. How long you been in America?"

"Almost three years now."

"Is that all? You're a smart boy. Good-looking, too," he said. "All you need is a haircut. Never mind. It's nice long. On you it looks good. You ought to get it singed, though, to shape it. I got a wop barber on Mulberry Street who'll do it for a dime. You got a dime?"

"I make out okay."

He said, "So I understand," and wiped the sweat from his face and neck with a handkerchief. He was wearing a stiff shirt with rubber cuffs and no collar. In his right hand he had a walking stick with a gold handle. The rumor was that he had brained a Chinaman on Mott Street with it in a fight over a Polish girl.

"I like a kid with a good head on his shoulders," he said. "Where you from?"

"You never heard of it."

"Try me."

"Umersk."

"You're right," he said. "Where's that?"

"About halfway between Zhitomir and Kiev," I told him. "And you?"

"Me?" He laughed. "I was born the minute I stepped off the boat at Castle Gardens."

He lit a cigar and the flare of the match was reflected in his eyes; they were pale blue. Blowing the smoke from his nose, he said, "They tell me your folks are dead."

"That's right."

"No brothers or sisters?"

"Nobody but me."

"You're better off."

Just at that moment, there was the squeal of the ungreased axle of a pushcart and the jingle of bells from the street.

I said, "I know it," and he laid a hand on my arm. A diamond ring glittered on his pinky. In the street, the peddler cried out in Yiddish, "Buy, Jews, buy!" He sold dried fruit, I remember.

Before he walked off, swinging that stick, Schlifka bought a pound of figs for a dime. "A little something for the girls on Allen Street," he said.

I wondered where he got his information about me. Mrs. Tauber, my landlady, would have spit in his eye, and there was no one else in the building, where I'd lived only three months, who knew I spoke English.

But the next morning, at work, I suddenly thought, I once told Hannah Isaacs, and put my steam iron down on the red-hot stove. A burning coal shot a yellow flame through the grate. In the front room, tailors, basters, and finishers bent over their rented sewing machines. A girl wearing a pleated skirt and a blouse with a high collar made her way down the aisle with a bundle of cut work in her arms. My iron hissed. I thought, Hannele and Schlifka? No, that ain't possible, but it was as if the heat had already fused them together in the back of my mind.

As soon as I got home, I had my supper—a piece of herring on a slice of black bread. The cup of coffee made me sweat. Hannele and her father lived in the back apartment, to the right, on the other side of the stairs. Every time the toilet in the hallway was flushed, I looked out the door. Finally, at about eight, when the water gushed and gurgled again in the pipes, I caught the eye of the locksmith from the second floor who was her old man's best friend. He buttoned up his fly and asked, "Something I can do for you?"

"Is Hannele at home?"

"Hannele's gone away," he said.

That night I waited on the stoop until ten for Schlifka to show up again. It was very hot. Mrs. Tauber was wearing her kimono; Feibush, the greenhorn, was in his undershirt. He had broad shoulders for a Jew. You could tell from the way he kept pulling on his chin that he had recently shaved off his beard.

While I watched the street, they talked in Yiddish with strong Ukrainian accents about Odessa: the Moldavanka district, some park near an avenue lined with poplar trees, Import Square. Mrs. Tauber said, "I miss the sea." An ambulance clanged by, drawn by two white horses; their hooves struck sparks from the cobblestones. Feibush must have asked her something about her husband, because then I heard her say, "No, he's been dead three years," as I got to my feet and went down the stairs.

I started out to buy a hard roll for breakfast in the

bakery on the corner of Hester Street; instead I made a left and kept going for another block. I suppose I had hopes of running into Schlifka on his home ground: under the El, on Allen Street, where it was always dark. In any case, I headed uptown. Now and then, in the light from an open store, I could make out a face: a Gypsy, with a gold ring in one ear, who was smoking a cigarette; a bearded Jew. On a fire escape, a girl put down a kerosene lamp with a tin shade. She had long hair. There was a pillow under her arm. The downtown express roared overhead. I passed the Russian steam bath and the shop that sold white linen shrouds, brass candlesticks for the Sabbath, and little bags of earth, tied with string, from the Holy Land. A hot moist wind was blowing. There was a smell of rotten fruit from the gutter.

On the corner of Broome Street, I sneaked upstairs to the Syrian coffeehouse on the second floor. The fat Syrian who owned the joint had tossed me out of there twice that summer before I had a chance to see the belly dancer do her stuff. This time I saw a woman on her knees in the center of a room. Her head was thrown back; a necklace of silver coins dangled between her naked breasts. She squeezed them together. Even now, after all these years, that sticks in my mind.

What completely escapes me is how and where I met Schlifka again. I know it was the following Saturday evening because I have a distinct memory, at one point, of hearing a verse from the hymn that marks the end of the Sabbath through the open window of a shul:

At the close of the Day of Rest
Deliver thy people;
Send us Elijah . . .

It might have been from the old Beth Hamidrash Hagadol on Norfolk Street, the one that used to be a church. Schlifka hummed the tune under his breath and said, "That takes me way back."

"Where to?"

"I already told you. Another life."

"Did you go to shul on Shabbes?"

"Not only that, but I studied Gemara as well."

"Where? In a yeshiva?"

"No, at a Gemara cheder."

"Me too."

"We got a lot in common," he said.

"Were you a good student?"

"By the time I was eleven, I knew the Mesachet Shabbes by heart."

"Then how come you didn't go to a yeshiva?"

"That's a long story," he said. "And very sad. What about you?"

"Mine's a long story, too."

We wound up on Allen Street, opposite the Rivington Street station.

"I got me a room here on the second floor," he said, in front of an open doorway. "This is where I green out my new girls."

A gas jet burned in the hallway; the glass mantel was chipped. There was a dead rat in the big puddle on the black-and-white-tile floor.

A little way up the block, outside a saloon, Schlifka went on, "Gimme a girl, any girl, up in that room for a week or ten days, and I promise you this: when I spit in her face, she'll call it rain. Understand me? No, you can't. You're too young. Well, then, I'll try and put it to you another way."

He thumped me on the chest with the gold handle of his walking stick: the head of a dog with a long muzzle and pointed ears. "Our rabbis teach us to discover our *'shoresh nishama.'* You know what that means?"

"Sure."

"What?"

"What's *'shoresh'* again in English? It's on the tip of my tongue."

"Root."

"Yeah, that's it. I got it now. It means 'the root of the soul.' "

"That's right," he said. "Very good. For instance, Levi Yitzhak . . . no . . . the Apter, as you know, had the same root as the High Priest in Jerusalem, who was a very holy man. Well, believe it or not, I've discovered minc. It came to me in a flash one night up there in that room with a girl. And you know who it is?"

"No."

"Take a guess," he said. "I'll give you a hint. I seen a bone once, from his thigh, in a show at Coney Island. It was as tall as me."

"I don't know what you're talking about."

"I'm talking about Og," he said, "the root of my soul."

"Who?"

"Og," he repeated. "Don't you remember?" He quoted the Hebrew in an exaggerated singsong voice, " 'Behold, his bedstead was a bedstead of iron. And nine cubits was its length, and four cubits its breadth.' "

"I remember," I said. "He was the king of Bashan."

"Right again. And, like the rabbis tell us, he had a thousand wives. As a matter of fact, every girl in that town, on the day she turned twelve years old, became his slave. She went to live in the palace that afternoon. And that very night, apart from her jewelry—which was made from iron, too—she had to strip herself naked and bring the king his supper and a glass of beer. But if he liked what he saw, she didn't last long."

"Why not?"

He bit off the tip of a cigar, spit it out, and said, "A guy that size?"

We burst out laughing together.

"You got a sense of humor," he said. "You're okay. Do you like cigars?"

"I don't know. I never tried one."

"Try one of these. It's a genuine Havana—the best. It set me back four bits."

"For one cigar?"

"Nothing's too good for Schlifka and his pals."

"Are we pals?"

"We could be," he said, giving me a light. "Well, how do you like it?"

"I don't know yet."

"No, don't drag it quick, like a cigarette. Puff on it slow and easy," he said. "That's the way. Now lick the wrapper; that's the leaf on the outside. It tastes good, don't it? That's how you can tell a good Havana. This wrapper is called *Vuelta Abajo.* That's Spanish; it's the best money can buy. Now puff on it again. Enjoy the smell."

"How come you know Spanish?"

"I get around," he said. "Well, how do you like it now?"

"It makes me dizzy."

"That's because you drag on it, like a cigarette."

"Maybe so, but it ain't for me," I told him, tossing it in the gutter.

He laughed again and said, "You make up your mind very fast."

"I know what I like."

"How would you like to make yourself ten bucks?"

"Very much."

"With no questions asked."

"That all depends."

"No," he said. "Not for ten bucks."

He reached into his pocket, pulled out a wad, and peeled off one of the bills. "This is for you," he said. "All you have to do is tell me when Hannah Isaacs comes home to her papa."

"Is Hannah Isaacs one of your girls?"

He stuffed the bill down the front of my shirt and pinched me on the right cheek. There was a gust of wind. A sheet, strung between two fire escapes, flapped above his head. The shiny hair stayed slicked down. After we made the deal and shook on it, the wind changed and I caught a whiff of his cigar.

2

THE LAST THING Schlifka said to me was "You see that Hungarian joint right across the street? The one with the swinging doors? That's Kertesz's, where I usually grab a bite to eat. Try me there after midnight, any night, as soon as she shows her face."

"Are you Hungarian?"

He gave me another pinch on the cheek, crossed the street, and went through those swinging doors. On the stoop behind me, a woman was grating horseradish on a machine padlocked to the iron banister. "Two for a penny," she said in Yiddish. "How about it?"

"No, thanks."

"What's a penny to a boy who has so much money?"

"How do you know how much money I have?"

"I've got eyes, haven't I?"

I walked up the block, ducked into an empty doorway, fished out the ten-dollar bill, and carefully folded it up. Then I took off my right shoe and stuck the wad in my sock, under my big toe.

I wore the sock to bed. It made me think of the winter nights, when I bundled up under a woolen blanket, in my socks, my pants, and my only sweater. I'll blow myself to a quilt stuffed with goose feathers, I thought. Or better yet, a coat. I turned over. A warm coat made more sense; I could sleep in it as well. That's it, I decided, closing my eyes. I'll buy me a warm coat for the winter.

I couldn't bring myself to go shopping for a couple of days. The ten-dollar bill was the first I ever owned. Again and again, I sneaked off to the toilet at work and looked at it. On one side, was a blue seal and an engraving of McKinley wearing a wing collar. His name was underneath—I had no idea who he was. On the other was a woman with long feathers stuck in her hair. I took her for a Red Indian.

At noon, on Tuesday, I counted up the finished cloaks on my rack and realized I was behind in my work. I skipped lunch to make it up. And that evening, on my way to the elevator, Rabinowitz, the foreman, said to me in his Americanized Yiddish, "I want a word with you."

The elevator came and went. "I got my eye on you in that toilet," he said. "You better watch your step."

He started to say something else; instead, he coughed twice into the dirty handkerchief against his lips and brought up a lot of phlegm. He had weak lungs, exactly like my father, whom he had hired as an assistant presser fresh off the boat almost three years before. He cleared his throat, which made him cough again.

"It's nothing," he said. "Only a cold." But I could tell from his eyes that he was thinking about my father, too.

They knew each other years ago in Zhitomir, where they belonged to the Tailors' Shul; over here, they were members of the same burial society on East Broadway. The elevator came back—it rattled—and behind the dirty handkerchief, Rabinowitz said, "Don't take advantage of me."

The next morning I waited until he was on the other side of the room, with his back to me, before I put my steaming iron down on the stove and unwrapped the wet rag from my right hand. Then, in the dim light over the toilet bowl, I fixed those long feathers, the blue seal, and the wing collar in my mind for good. The toilet was clogged; the stench made me open the door a crack. I turned the bill over again and memorized the spelling of "McKinley." Then I stuck it in my pocket. "You ain't the last," I said aloud.

I said it again that night, when I bought a second-hand corduroy coat, lined with sheepskin, for two and a half dollars from a peddler on Broome Street. We haggled under a street lamp for an hour.

Afterward, I noticed that there was a full moon. I remember it because, on the next block, I spotted Feibush and Mrs. Tauber out for a stroll. The moonlight was shining on her long, thick hair, which fell in tapering ringlets on her bare neck.

In all this time, there was no sign of Hannah at the house. By the end of the week, though, I found out a lot more about her old man. He wasn't just a broken-down Hebrew teacher who charged ten cents a lesson to the kids in the neighborhood. I overheard the locksmith call him "Rabbi" on the stairs. And exactly at midnight, every night, he'd open the door of his apartment and take off his shoes and socks. His forehead was smeared with something black and greasy; probably ashes from the kitchen stove. He pulled a pillowcase over his head, and got down on his hands and knees. It's true—I watched him through my keyhole twice in a row. He stretched out his arms, pressed his forehead against the floor, and began to pray out loud. That's what first tipped me off: the Hebrew echoing from the tiled hall: "O God, the heathen have come into thine inheritance; thy holy temple have they defiled."

I also discovered that he couldn't afford to buy himself cigarettes. He bummed three in two nights on the stoop from Mrs. Tauber, who smoked the same brand: Tolstoys—Russian-type cigarettes, with black tobacco and cardboard mouthpieces, which were manufactured in America. The next time she offered him one without being asked.

That was at five-thirty, Sunday morning, on the first floor. She and I were leaving for work; the old man had just come through the door. One of his payess, soaked with sweat, dangled below his ear; the other was tucked up under his fur hat. He was carrying a paper bag.

After taking two quick drags, he said, "Not much like *makhorka,* is it? That's all I ever smoked in Kiev.

It was cheap and good. But there's no use complaining. This is the time, you know, when the face of the Shekinah is dark; when she tastes the other side."

He pinched off the lighted end of the cigarette, which kept burning on the floor, and added, "I'll save the rest for after a glass of tea."

Mrs. Tauber took me by the arm going down the stoop. "What was he talking about?" she asked. "Do you know?"

"I'm not sure."

"He's crazy."

The sun off the sidewalk hit me in the face. I walked her as far as Stanton Street, where she worked as a sewing-machine operator for a shirtwaist contractor. His name was Riegler; he got his start as a strikebreaker in the famous cloakmakers' strike two years before. I mention him only because Mrs. Tauber gossiped about him the whole time. He carried a revolver; his wife had diabetes; he was playing around with an Italian salesgirl at Hearn's. At the last minute, just before I caught my trolley, she added, "Wherever she is, Hannele is better off."

I pumped Mrs. Tauber about the old man after supper. We were still at the kitchen table, between the bathtub and the stove, waiting for the samovar to boil.

"Is he really a rabbi?" I asked. "Then how come he teaches Hebrew to kids for a living? And why does he stay out all night? Where does he go? Do you know?"

"It's a long story," she said, lighting a cigarette. "One thing at a time. Yes, he's a rabbi. Or he was, in Kiev, before he came here. That, by the way, was only nine months ago. He and Hannele were brought over—in a cabin, no less, second-class—by the congregation of the shul between Ludlow and Essex Streets. You know the one I mean? The storefront with the curtains in the window, on the lefthand side, as you go toward Seward Park.

"Most of the congregation was from Kiev, too, and about two and a half years ago they decided they wanted a rabbi from their hometown. Someone with a reputation for being pious, and a scholar. In short, the old man, who'd made a name for himself by publishing a translation of selections from the Zohar in Yiddish—along with a commentary.

"The president of the shul—a milliner by the name of Appelbaum—wrote him a letter; he wrote back. In no time, everything was settled. The trouble was, it took the congregation two more years to raise the money for those two second-class boat tickets, plus the train fare from Kiev to Hamburg, and the other expenses.

"By then, as you can guess, they were no longer such greenhorns. Appelbaum, for example, had learned English at the Educational Alliance. Some of the other men trimmed their beards. They all cut off their payess. According to Hannele, who gave me all these details, Appelbaum's mouth dropped open when he got his first look at the old man coming off the ferry from Ellis Island. I don't wonder. He was wearing that moth-eaten fur hat of his—the one he had on this morning; it's fox, I think—and, of course, his black caftan, with a piece of rope tied around his waist. Also felt boots, like a Russian peasant. He still wears them in the winter.

"Anyhow, a week or so later, after mincha on a Saturday night, Appelbaum presented him with a pair of high-button calfskin shoes, a silk top hat, a Prince Albert with a velvet collar, and an umbrella —one with an ivory handle. The old man refused to put on the shoes, the hat, and the coat, but thanked him for the umbrella, as it happened to be raining.

" 'You don't understand, Rabbi,' Appelbaum said. 'They go together. You're in America now. This is what American rabbis wear.'

"The old man handed him back the shoes and said, 'And what else will be expected of me in America? That, God forbid, I cut off my payess? Put a razor to my beard?'

"To make a long story short, one word led to another, and the old man quit on the spot. Hannele, who was sitting in the back with the other women, burst out crying. In addition to everything else, Appelbaum had promised her a job."

The samovar whistled; two glowing coals, forced down by a heap of gray ash, dropped on the tray. We each drank two glasses of the steaming tea, one right after the other, while she said, "Appelbaum, naturally, was livid. On his recommendation the congregation was out—I don't know how much money: a small fortune. But I'll say this for him, he was a man of his word. He got Hannele that job. She worked at home, willowing ostrich feathers for women's hats. Do you know anything about that kind of work?"

"No."

"I have to describe it for you—so you can appreciate the rest of the story."

She lit another cigarette. "It's the way to make

short feathers—cheap ones—into one long plume. You have to knot them together, with tiny knots, and then shape the whole thing with a scissors. You're paid by the knot. I forget the going rate—something like thirty or forty knots for a penny. Hannele worked in the kitchen, twelve to fourteen hours a day. The floor was covered with snips from the feathers. After four or five months, her eyes started to go. The lids became irritated and puffy; she began seeing double."

With a fresh lump of sugar on her tongue, like a Russian, Mrs. Tauber sipped the tea. Then she took a drag on her cigarette.

"The rest of the story, as you've probably guessed, is about that crazy old man. He picked up a little money giving Hebrew lessons, as you know, and spent the rest of his time in shul or poring over the Zohar at home. Three volumes, bound in red Moroccan leather, no less, that he brought with him from Kiev. One of them was called *Idra Rabba,* I remember. I once asked him what, in God's name, he was reading all day.

"Then, at the beginning of winter, right after the first snow, I happened to notice that Hannele had a slice of black bread and a pickle for supper two or three nights in a row. No butter, mind you, or cheese. Not even a salted herring. Her father drank three or four glasses of tea—but without sugar or lemon. I figured things were very bad, and didn't think too much about it. After all, there was nothing I could do to help. I was still paying off my husband's headstone at the time—two dollars a week—and had trouble making ends meet myself.

"But I was wrong. It was the old man's fault. God only knows what gave him the idea—the snow, maybe, and his felt boots. Or those shoes that Appelbaum had offered him that night in shul. "To tell you the truth, the whole business was a story straight out of one of those two-kopek Yiddish chapbooks for women that I ate up like potato pancakes when I was a kid."

"What did the old man do?"

"He took away almost all of Hannele's wages, to begin with, and scraped together every cent he could. She was only too glad to help; she worked an hour or two extra every night. Her eyes filled up with pus; they were stuck together in the mornings when she woke up. Finally, at the end of December, he'd saved up enough: three dollars and a little change."

"Enough for what? I don't understand."

"For a pair of boots, believe it or not. He bought a brand-new pair of all-wool, blue felt boots, with rubber soles, for two dollars and eighty cents."

"For himself?"

"No, no. He took them to the Russian steam bath on Allen Street that Friday afternoon. Then, when he was sure no one was watching, he went through the piles of clothing in the dressing room, found the pair of shoes in the worst shape—ones with cardboard soles—and exchanged the boots for them.

"Ostrovsky, the locksmith from the second floor, was with him; he guarded the door. The old man made him swear never to tell anyone else, but he blabbed it to me the very next day." She laughed. "He didn't know if the boots fit."

"Did you tell the old man off?"

"Believe me, it crossed my mind, but what was the use? Hannele was his; she belonged to him body and soul—or so I thought. One night, right after we became friends, she told me that she had irregular periods; sometimes she skipped a month entirely; at others, she menstruated every fifteen days. 'I never know when,' she said, and so help me God, there were tears in her puffy eyes. Why? Because, to be on the safe side, her father never touched her. He dropped things into her hand—the house key, for instance, when she had to go out and deliver her plumes to the contractor. Did she complain? Not on your life. Just the opposite, in fact. She always whispered, 'Thank you, Papa,' in a way that gave me goose pimples . . .

"No, I knew there was no sense in sticking my nose in between them, as the saying goes. This spring, by accident, I found out that the old man was up to his old tricks—but with a new twist. He works, without pay, for the Podol Burial Society on East Broadway."

"I know where that is."

"One of the finishers, where I work, is a member. Last May, when his youngest kid was run over by a beer truck on Second Avenue, he told me that the old man came to the house and washed the body. That's probably what he was doing last night."

"What about a taharah board? Doesn't he use one?"

"What's that?"

A drop of water from the faucet splashed in the iron bathtub; the gas meter clicked above the stove.

It burned almost anything: coke, soft coal, corn cobs, wood. Mrs. Tauber used soft coal. It stayed hot enough from supper to fog up my empty glass.

Finally, I said, "Papa belonged to one on the same block—the Khevreh Kadisha of Zhitomir. The old man who washed his body was from Ozerne, though. Actually, he wasn't that old; there was something the matter with his spine. He was all hunched over, but his beard was as black as coal. I warmed the water for him, on the stove, in a big iron kettle I borrowed from our landlady, Mrs. Litvinoff; we were living in her parlor on Eldridge Street at the time. Then I had to go next door, to the Rivkins, and borrow an egg and a glass of wine. I was only ten when Mama died; I had no idea what they were for. I asked the hunchback twice, 'Why do you need an egg and a glass of wine?' but he didn't answer me."

The gas meter clicked again, but, like the drop of water in the tap, my memories gathered for another moment. Then I said, "I peeked in the parlor, though, about an hour later—but just for a second. I couldn't help myself. It was the first time in my whole life I saw Papa naked; he was always very strict about that. He was propped up, on his feet, on a wooden plank, about six feet long—less—and three feet wide, at an angle, against the wall next to the cot."

"The taharah board?"

"It was made from pine; there was a knothole between his ankles. His fingers were spread apart. Just before he died, after he plucked at the blanket, he clenched them tight. When I saw them opened again

—I don't know why—I slammed the door and ran downstairs. We were on the fifth floor."

Mrs. Tauber said, "What did he die from?"

"Pneumonia. He woke up with a chill one morning, about a week and a half before last Pesach, and lived eight more days. The doctor thought he would make it, but late in the afternoon of the sixth day, when he coughed up some blood, he made me put a basin of water and a towel on the chair by his bed so that the Angel of Death could clean off his knife before he used it. That's the custom we have in Umersk to make things easier."

"In Odessa, too."

"He was very scared."

She asked me something else, but I didn't catch it; I was wondering again about the egg, the glass of wine, and the naked corpse with spread fingers, propped up on the board against the wall.

I ran into Schlifka again at the beginning of the week because of the heat wave. Mrs. Tauber slept on her fire escape; I tried the roof, which was jammed. Tuesday night Feibush saved me a spot under the chimney, where I spread a newspaper on the sticky tar paper, stretched out with my hands behind my head, and listened to him talk. He asked if Mrs. Tauber ever mentioned him, whether she saw other men. "No," I said. "Neither; not as far as I know."

"Did you ever meet her husband?"

"No."

"She loved him," he said. "She told me so. Which means only one thing."

"What's that?"

"Sooner or later, she'll get married again."

The wind, off the East River, had an oily smell. He said, "Also, she wants children—at least two, she says. Boys or girls, one of each—it makes no difference to her. 'Me too,' I told her. 'It's the same.' Her first husband was a baker, you know. He did pretty well."

"And you?"

"I was a cabinetmaker in Odessa. And a good one, too, if I say so myself, with a shop of my own on Bolshaya Arnautskaya Street—a whole basement. I worked in teak, oak, and pine. Imported teak was my specialty. It's hard, like iron; you have to be very strong to carve it. I made some beautiful chests from that teak. Not only in the Russian style, mind you, but Japanese as well. They were very popular after the war."

"And now?"

"Now, of course, it's a different story," he said, and in spite of myself, I got a kick out of hearing that he had to hire himself out on street corners as a carpenter, doing odd jobs, for a day or two at a time. He shingled roofs in Brooklyn, repaired the benches in a shul on Delancey Street.

"If I were you, I wouldn't count too much on marrying Mrs. Tauber," I said. "She won't settle for a greenhorn carpenter. A woman like that can have any man she wants."

The shadow of the chimney, cast by the remaining moon, covered his face. It took me a minute to realize that he was asleep. I closed my eyes. The groans, the oily smell, Feibush's arm flung suddenly across my chest, reminded me of coming across in steerage on the *Kaiser Wilhelm der Grosse.* Some kid behind me burst out laughing in a high-pitched voice. Feibush began to snore. I took his arm off my chest, got to my feet, and decided to go for a walk.

In those days, as you walked west on Hester Street, there was a drugstore on the righthand side with a bottle of red water in the window. Schlifka was coming out as I passed. He said, "Long time no see," and we shook hands. Ahead of us, at the end of the block, was one of those iron stanchions that held up the El. We got close enough for me to make out the rivets and the rust in the headlights of a car before he added, "How come?"

"I had nothing to tell you. Hannele never showed."

"Are you sure?"

"I'm positive."

"She's found another guy," he said. "I'll bet on it. I should have known."

In the middle of Allen Street, a truck horse had collapsed in its harness and died; the gray belly was swollen.

Schlifka said, "But who? And where did she meet him? This beats everything."

The cop at the curb touched his forefinger to his helmet; he had on white gloves. There were two gold stripes on his cuff.

"Hello, Dooley," Schlifka said. "How's tricks?"

"I got no complaints."

"How's the Mrs.?"

"She complains all the time. She's got the arthritis very bad."

"I'm sorry to hear it."

"That's the way it goes," Dooley said, swinging his billy at the end of a thong tied to his belt.

Schlifka said, "He's on the take, that mick son of a bitch. He costs me fifteen bucks a week."

"For what?"

"You'd be surprised." He took my arm. "You and me got business, too," he said. "We got to talk some more."

"Whatever you say."

At the last frame building before Stanton Street, he opened the front door. "Come on up here with me—it'll only take a minute. Then we'll grab a bite to eat."

"What's here?"

"All my girls, with their mama."

"Their mama?"

"Yetta, who looks after them for me. All the girls call her Mama."

On the first floor, I heard a sewing machine, and a man singing loudly in Yiddish,

Don't just stand there.
Unite, comrades.
Our might is in our numbers,
Like the waves of the sea . . .

In an open doorway, on the third, there was a cobbler working by candlelight. The curved knife flashed in his hand. On the fourth, I was startled because Schlifka spoke Yiddish to the fat woman who answered the door.

"Did you get it?" she asked him.

"Right here."

"It's about time. Rosa's climbing the walls."

In the smoky room behind her, the floor was covered with burlap sacks. I watched a girl in a ruffled petticoat scratch a rash on her neck until Schlifka said, "Charge her five bucks for it," and caught my attention again. There was a glass vial, with brown pills, in his right hand.

"Five?"

"She owes me," he said. "What good is she on this stuff? She doesn't work any more. Either she's climbing the walls or she sleeps. Do you know how much money she made last week?"

"Twenty bucks."

"A girl her age, with those looks, ought to be able to bring in twice that, easy. One of these days, I'm going to throw her out, in the gutter, where she belongs."

The girl scratched; a man who had been sitting on the wooden bench in the far corner to the left stood up.

"Keep your pants on," the girl said.

"You're from the Ukraine, too," I told Schlifka, when we were on the street again.

"You found me out."

"Whereabouts?"

"Well, I was born in Berdichev, but lived in Kiev until I was eleven. Down by the river, on Shechekovitskaya Street, in Podol, as a matter of fact; not too far from Hannele and her old man. They lived near the Lubyankovka, where my poor mama and papa are buried. Hannele's mama, too. We had something in common the first time we met."

"When was that?"

"Nosy, ain't you?"

"Yeah."

He laughed and said, "Well, if you must know, I picked her up one afternoon last winter—toward the end of December, I think—on Canal Street, outside Jarmulowsky's bank. It was pouring; raining cats and dogs. She had a gunny sack filled with her precious ostrich feathers; I had an umbrella. That was that."

"Did you meet her often?"

"That ain't neither here nor there," he said. "What's important, right now, is to find out where her new boy friend's got her hid. And that's up to you."

"How do I do that?"

"The same as before: keep your eyes open around the house. Only this time, watch her old man very carefully. Get chummy with him, if you can. Find out if he's heard from her. I know that dame. Sooner or later, she'll come back to see him; sooner, unless I miss my guess."

"And then what?"

"Follow her."

"I don't know," I said. "That's a lot more than I bargained for."

"What'd you have in mind to make up the difference?"

"I'll have to think about it."

"I'll give you five bucks the minute you tell me where she's at."

"No," I said. "In advance."

"Half now and half then."

"All of it now."

He poked his stick at an orange peel on the sidewalk. "Okay," he said. "You win. Have it your way. You got yourself another deal. Come on. We'll have a drink on it."

We each had three, one right after the other, at Kertesz's; three shots of bourbon at one of the tables in the back covered with oilcloth. The waiter, who had a bum left leg, dragged his foot in the sawdust to and from the bar. Schlifka called him Janos and, after we polished off the last round, asked him about somebody by the name of Zsuzya.

"She's better, Red. Thanks," he said.

"Glad to hear it. Send her my regards."

"I'll do that."

"Now, tell us what's good tonight. Me and my pal is starved."

"Have the goulash," Janos said.

I said, "Is that what they call you? Red?"

"Only my pals," Schlifka said. "Now how about it? The goulash okay with you?"

"I don't know. What's goulash? Is it pork?"

"Why? Are you kosher?"

"No," I said. "Not any more."

"The goulash tonight is veal," Janos said.

"I want something with pork in it," I said. "I never tasted pork."

"Well, we have Bakonyi pork tonight," Janos said. "That's thin slices, with mushrooms, from the leg. It's good, but the goulash is better."

"Bring me the pork," I said.

"Suit yourself."

He dragged his foot through the sawdust. The face of the man leaning over the bar was blurred. Schlifka said, "The veal in this joint ain't kosher, neither," and to bring him into focus, I had to squint. He was rolling the end of an unlit cigar on his tongue. The back of his hand was covered with hair; there was a tuft on each finger between the knuckle and the first joint.

I said, "Did you ever see anybody kill a pig?"

"Never," he said. "Why?"

"I did once, when I was a kid in Umersk. It was right after Succos, the year before Mama died. The pig was a whatchamacallit—a female. What do you call a female pig in English?"

He said without interest, "Search me," and lit his cigar.

"Well, whatever it is, she was huge; as big as a house. All black, you know, with long hair, as black as night, except for her big teats. They were pink. She belonged to Makhno, who made horseshoes and sometimes fixed wheels; things like that. What's the English word for one of those?"

"A blacksmith."

"Right," I said. "That was our Makhno; a blacksmith, with no eyebrows. His eyebrows were burned off from sparks. Where was I? Never mind, I remember: the pig. Actually Makhno comes first; that is, his daughter does. He had this daughter, you see, who was getting married to the local priest. All the Russians in town were invited to the wedding. Makhno decided to feed them the pig. When I found out, I took my life in my hands and sneaked off to see her killed. Nikodomich, the butcher, was in the Russian part of town, you see, where they had wooden sidewalks. It was no joke, believe me, for a Jew to get caught over there, particularly near the church. But I took the chance, anyway."

"Why?"

"I'm coming to that in a minute. Give me time."

"Well, then, go ahead."

"I can't," I said. "Would you believe it? I forget again where I was."

"Near the church," Schlifka said.

"Oh, I got by the church okay, and the Korpus, too, on the Platz where the Cossacks lived. We had Orenburg Cossacks in Umersk; they had blue stripes on their pants. On their caps, too; blue . . ."

The man at the bar, with the blurred face, yelled, "And a schooner to go, you hear?"

"It was worth it," I said. "I looked through a hole in the fence and saw everything: the kettle over the roaring fire, the fresh straw on the ground, a wooden bucket, and the knife. I got a good look at the knife just before Nikodomich slipped it into his boot. It had a bone handle and a blade, I swear, that was half as long as my arm. The pig was facing me. She had tiny eyes. Then she grunted and turned away, toward the bucket. Nikodomich came up to her from the side, bent down, grabbed an ear and a back leg, just above the hoof, and with one heave threw her on her back.

"Well, you can imagine. She kicked and tried to get up again. The bucket was knocked over. But before she had a chance, Nikodomich stood over her head, with one leg on either side, and pulled the knife out of his boot. Then he stuck the blade in her throat. It went in right up to that bone handle and she screamed. I never heard anything like it. It sounded like a human being—a woman. There was no blood, though; would you believe that? Not a drop, until Nikodomich pulled the knife out. Then—whoosh—he had to wipe it from his eyes.

"One of them Cossacks, who was walking his horse on the Platz, spotted me on the way back. I had to run for my life, but I didn't care. I saw the pig get up. She even managed to take a step before she slipped in her own blood, on the wet straw, and went down again—plop—on her right side. I wouldn't have missed that for the world."

"Hey, Janos, what's the English word for a lady pig?" Schlifka asked.

"You got me there," Janos said, as he put the plates and the knives and forks on the table. "In Hungarian we say *koca.* Be careful. Them plates is hot."

"What's these things?" I asked him.

"Those are dumplings."

"They taste very good."

"Never mind," Schlifka said. "How about the pork?"

"I like it," I said, through a mouthful. "It's spicy, but good."

"Bring us a couple of beers," Schlifka said.

After the coffee, he picked his teeth with a sliver from a wooden match and asked, "But why all the fuss about some pig? I don't get it."

"I told you. She belonged to Makhno."

"So what?"

"He turned her loose in our garden. We had this little garden, you see, with a fence around it, in front of our house, where Mama grew red cabbages. They came up in the fall, just before the first frost. Mama made borscht from them and sometimes even holishkes for Shabbes. She'd stuff them with beef marrow and chopped onions. That don't sound like much, I know, but it meant a lot to us. Most of the time, we lived on black bread, salted herring, and talakno, like the peasants, made from oats mixed with cold water. Did you ever eat that stuff?"

"I ate it," Schlifka said.

"Well, then you know how much them cabbages meant to us. Then, like I said, Makhno decided to fatten up his pig for his daughter's wedding. He'd never made trouble for the Jews before; as a matter of fact, he was friendly, as peasants go, even when he got drunk. But he turned that pig loose in our garden, just the same. It was very early in the morning, I remember, a cool fall day, but clear—no rain. The first thing I heard was this crash as the fence caved in. I jumped out of bed and ran to the window. The pig was already in the cabbages, gobbling them up one by one.

"Before I knew what I was doing, I ran outside and picked up a stone. Papa was right behind me; Makhno was standing in the road, on the other side of the busted fence, with one of them iron things in his hand; what you use to pick up the red-hot horseshoe and dunk it in the water. Then Mama, who'd come to the doorway, screamed, but I threw the stone at the pig as hard as I could.

"It hit her right behind the ear. She picked up her head. Her nose was covered with dirt. There was a cabbage in her mouth. Makhno waved that iron thing in the air and yelled my father's name at the top of his lungs. The next thing I know, both of them are standing there, in the dusty road, with their heads together, talking like old friends. Papa knew some Russian. His hands were clasped behind his back. He was also in his nightshirt, by the way, and bare feet. But, like always, there was a yarmulke on his head. Then he nods, comes back through the hole in the fence, and grabs me by the arm.

" 'His honor wants you to apologize,' he says, and as soon as the words are out of his mouth, Makhno bursts out laughing. And, with his head thrown back, he laughs and laughs.

"I asked my father, 'What's so funny, Papa?' but he yanked me by the arm, and while Mama watched from the doorway, he made me go over to that pig and apologize in a loud voice."

There was a clatter of silverware from the table on my right, where now, without squinting, I could see a very old man with a long white mustache pick up a spoon and rub it against his sleeve. Janos served him soup and said something in Hungarian. The lips behind the sparse white hairs barely moved, but Janos went, "Ah," and called out to Schlifka over the steaming bowl, "The word in English is 'sow.' "

"How do you know?"

"Mr. Lukacs here is an educated man."

3

IN MY ROOM, before I went to sleep, I put aside the two bucks for my rent, which I gave Mrs. Tauber every Friday evening after I got paid. What got to me was that I still had ten bucks left: two five-dollar bills, under my toes, in my right sock. That was two weeks' wages.

I got eight cents for pressing a tweed jacket and a woolen skirt. The iron weighed fourteen pounds; it was one of those things you knew. I used two of them. There was always one heating up on the stove. I worked at a big table opposite Spiegel, another presser, who'd been at it for six years. His right shoulder was three inches lower than his left; the forefinger of his right hand reached his knee.

"What is it?" he asked me Wednesday afternoon. "What's the matter with you?"

"Nothing."

I'd been staring at him. He turned a skirt without pleats inside out, spread it on his board, covered the seam with a strip of canvas, and then reached into the tin pail on his right, squeezed the water from the brown sponge and swept it up and halfway down the canvas, leaving a wet trail. It went on and on: a continuous movement of the lowered shoulder, the elongated arm, the hand wrapped in a wet rag. I saw the swollen blue veins on the inside of his wrist as he tossed the sponge back into the pail. When he picked up the iron, he grunted "Oy" under his breath, and a drop of sweat from his temple ran down the left side of his face; another hung from the tip of his nose.

On the way home, I bought a pack of Tolstoys—ten cigarettes for a nickel—in the hope of bumping into old man Isaacs on the stoop, in the hallways, or on the narrow stairs. No soap. At midnight, though, through the kitchen door, I heard him praying again.

I had another idea. On Friday afternoon, with the religious Jews in the shop, I quit work at four-thirty. And sure enough, I figured right: five minutes after I got home, with a lit cigarette in my mouth, I met the old man on the third floor, at the head of the stairs. His beard was damp; he'd just returned from a mikvah—the one on Essex Street, I think—where he prepared himself for the coming of the Sabbath by taking a bath.

He said, "I didn't know you smoked."

"Have one on me."

"No, thank you. I couldn't."

"Go ahead, Reb Isaacs. Take a couple. I insist."

"Well, maybe just two," he said. "The last before Shabbes, you understand."

He smoked the first in his open doorway. The ashes fell on his beard.

He said, "You want to know the truth? Going without a cigarette on Shabbes is the greatest sacrifice I have to make for my faith. Would you believe such a thing?"

"Why not? It was very hard for my father, too."

"I cheat."

"So did my father."

"Is that so?" he asked. "How?"

"Once in a while, in the toilet, he grabbed a puff on the sly."

"From a lit cigarette?"

"How else?"

"Ah," he said sadly. "Come in and see."

He turned up the gas in the kitchen, a roach scuttled under the icebox, and I had a glimpse of Hannele's brass bed in the next room; the torn mattress was stuffed with straw.

"What's the important thing?" he asked. "Not to light any fire on Shabbes, right? That's the Law. It says nothing about smoke, though, does it?"

"No."

"Then watch."

With the first cigarette, he lit the second, which he took from behind his ear. He dropped the burning butt on the floor, stepped on it, and reached for an empty milk bottle on the shelf above the stove. It was between two books bound in red leather.

"It's very simple," he said. "The mouth of the bottle, as you can see for yourself, is sealed with wax." He picked up a fork from the table. "All I have to do is make one hole in it—so! And then fill the bottle up with smoke, just like this."

On the table, by the bed, there was a little night lamp with a ruby glass shade and an amber comb. The shade was cracked.

"There," he said. "Now all you have to do is plug up the hole again with a little ball of wax, like this, until you want a puff."

"That's very clever."

"You think so? Do you really think that the Almighty is fooled by such things?"

"I don't know anything about the Almighty," I said.

"Don't you believe in God?"

"No."

"Or in the coming of the Messiah?"

"No."

"You don't believe that, as our sages have promised us, death will be swallowed up?"

"I'd like to believe in that," I said.

"Would you?"

"Very much."

"Yes," he said. "I see it in your eyes."

Another roach, the length of my finger, scurried up the wall behind him, over the peeling yellow paint, toward the shelf. The feelers waved in the air.

"Can you keep a secret?" the old man asked.

"Try me."

The feelers groped under the wood.

The old man, who leaned forward, whispered in my ear, "It'll be sooner than you think."

"Is that a fact? How do you know?"

He opened the door and I went into the hallway, where he whispered in my ear again, "Take my word for it. There are signs."

A glass shattered in the rear apartment. Tofetsky, the printer from Lemberg, yelled at his wife, "Don't put all the blame on me," and their three- or four-year-old son began to cry.

I had to raise my voice to the old man. "What kind of signs?"

The kid yowled. He must have been right by the door. The old man kept on whispering.

"I can't hear you," I said.

With his head to one side, and his wrinkled lids half closed, he was listening to the kid behind the door. Finally, very distinctly, he said, "In Kishinev, you know, during the pogrom, they hammered nails into the children's heads."

"Is that a sign?"

He answered me in Hebrew. " 'Shall there be evil in a city and the Lord hath not done it?' "

That evening, for the first time, Mrs. Tauber invited Feibush for supper.

"You too," she said, as I came in. "Come and sit down."

It was an afterthought; I noticed that there were only two plates and two glasses at the round table. They also noticed it and exchanged looks above the stuffed carp and the jug of homemade kvass, which Mrs. Tauber brewed from stale black bread.

"Over here," Feibush said. "Next to me."

"No, thanks. Maybe next time."

"No arguments. Sit down."

So I sat between them, on a three-legged stool, and shared the carp, the pot roast with candied carrots, the calf's-foot jelly, which was still warm, and a half a glass of the kvass. But that was all. Their conversation was beyond me. Who the hell was Dolly? Why did she walk out on her husband, the watchmaker, three days after they got married? What was so damn funny about that?

"Go ahead, laugh," Mrs. Tauber said. "But she can't help it. That's the way she was brought up."

"I can't help it, either," Feibush said. "It reminds me of the old story."

"Which?"

He leaned one elbow on the table, next to his empty glass, rubbed his chin, and asked, "What did our Father Adam say to our Mother Eve after they were kicked out of the Garden of Eden?"

"I give up," she said. "What?"

" 'You'd better stand back. I don't know how big this thing is going to get.' "

I said, "I'm dead. Excuse me," and went to my room, where I lay down on the folding iron cot in the dark. The warped door remained ajar. They were still laughing in the kitchen.

Afterward, I heard them clink their glasses together and Feibush sing in a surprisingly high voice,

Here, have a swig.
The rain has stopped.
The dove has gone
To build her nest

Between two sprigs of cedar
In the Lebanon . . .

Five or ten minutes after that, they left the apartment to go for a walk. I lit a candle in the dish I kept on top of my valise and, for the second time in a little less than a month, went into Mrs. Tauber's bedroom next door. A floorboard creaked, the candle flickered, and the shadow of the chiffonier—it had carved claw feet—jumped up and down on the wall.

I went through the second drawer, where she kept her underwear. There, between two folded corset covers, trimmed with lace, was a blue velvet sachet stuffed with dried rose petals. All I wanted was a smell.

I always slept late on Shabbes. At about nine-thirty, while I was having my second cup of coffee, Mrs. Tauber came into the kitchen and asked, "What're you doing with yourself today?"

"I don't know yet. I haven't decided. Why?"

"It's going to be a scorcher. How about you and me getting some fresh air?"

"Where's Feibush?"

"Working," she said. "He's got a job in the Bronx. How about it? I thought we'd go down by the river. What do you say?"

"Okay."

The East River was dark blue, almost black. From the Grand Street pier we watched the Brooklyn ferry move diagonally into its slip. The white swash broke against the pier heads and rushed through the pilings.

"Doesn't Feibush mind working on Shabbes?" I asked.

"No, not at all. He doesn't even think about it," Mrs. Tauber said. "He comes from a religious home, of course, but somehow it never took with him. There are people, you know, in the middle of a plague who never catch cholera. Who knows why? In the old country, to please his parents, he wore a beard and all the rest of it. But he never, for one minute, really believed that there was a God. He shrugs and says, 'It doesn't make any sense to me; it never has.' "

The swash was gone; the dark water still rose and fell against the pilings.

"It was very different for me," she said.

"Me too."

"Yes, I guessed as much."

A flock of gulls, with black-tipped wings, circled in the air above a garbage scow being pushed out to sea by a tug.

I said, "I believed in everything when I was a kid, until Mama died. That finished it for me."

"Why?"

"It's hard for me to explain."

The gulls shrieked. Mrs. Tauber said, "Death," and as we strolled south on Tompkins Street, along the river toward the Williamsburg Bridge, she told me about going to her first funeral when she was twelve years old.

At the beginning, I hardly listened; I think she said it was her uncle who'd died. Mostly, I was aware of a ringlet, swaying back and forth, on her sweaty neck, above her left breast. The strand of hair, which was unraveling, had an auburn tinge in the sunlight. And in the glare off the water her pupils were contracted. She had gray eyes; so far, I've neglected to mention those.

"It was muddy," she said. "Very hard to walk. One of the tombstones, near the entrance, had toppled over."

What used to be called a Mary Sugar Bum—an old female drunk—was passed out in the gutter between the two piers on East Street; she was almost bald. Mrs. Tauber lit a cigarette.

"Mama and I had to walk with the other women way ahead of the coffin," she said. "The men walked behind it—Papa, the rabbi, even my little brother, Feivel, who was only eight years old. There was an inch of water, maybe more, at the bottom of the open grave. When I saw that, I wanted to run back through the mud that reached my ankles and throw myself in Papa's arms.

" 'Stand still,' Mama told me. 'It's forbidden. The women must remain apart.'

" 'But why?' I asked.

" 'As punishment,' she said.

" 'For what?'

"And then she asked me, 'Why do we have to die?'

" 'I don't know,' I told her.

" 'Why do you think?' she said. 'May God forgive us; because of the sin of our Mother Eve.'

"My heart stopped. When the first spadeful of mud was thrown on the pine coffin in the grave, I almost fainted. Zelig had been a handsome man. He had beautiful blue eyes—too far apart—but the color of cornflowers. Now they would rot in his head. And why? All because of a woman, her willful disobedience to God. Her vanity.

"And wasn't I the same? I looked at the sky. It was all clouded over. Another spadeful of mud landed on the coffin. I couldn't breathe. Yes, I thought. It's true. May God forgive me, too. All I wanted from life was a new dress for Shabbes—one made out of white muslin—and fresh olive oil to smear on my hair.

"It began to drizzle. I shut my eyes and prayed, 'God in Heaven, Master of the Universe, forgive me. Help me. Humble me . . .' "

Opposite the Cleary Brothers warehouse, with two padlocks on the huge door, she added, "After that, for almost a year, I prayed in secret every day. Once, on Gluhaya Street, I scooped up a handful of dirt from the gutter and swallowed it. Another time I ate a live red spider."

We reached the pier, under the shadow of the bridge, where it was cool, and she went on, "None of it did any good. Something in me rebelled. I hated my brother—how I hated him!—for being a boy. Nothing was too good for him—the little snot. In the winter he slept on the stove in the parlor, the warmest spot in the house. Every Friday afternoon the rabbi came and quizzed him on what he had learned in cheder that week. And he was a good student; I had to admit that. He knew all the answers. Papa sat on the horsehair sofa and beamed. Mama always rewarded him with a lump of barley sugar the size of my fist. But nobody ever noticed me. I felt bewitched, under a spell, invisible, as if I were already in my grave. I swear to you that I was surprised to find that I still had a shadow or a reflection in a mirror."

She laughed. "As a matter of fact, as time went on, I looked at myself in the mirror more and more. I spent hours in front of the one on Mama's washstand. I was getting prettier every day, and I was proud of it. I particularly loved my hair; it shone without any olive oil. My neck was too long—I faced up to that—but so what? I had beautiful eyes and lips.

"One afternoon I locked the bedroom door and kissed the reflection of my lips again and again. My breath steamed up the glass. That made it look as if I were wearing a veil. I imagined that I was a bride—the Queen of Sheba, presented to King Solomon, who could only see her eyes and shining hair. After a while, as it got dark, I imagined that I was Solomon, too. Tall and handsome, like Papa, with a curly black beard that covered his chest." She laughed again. "I fell in love with myself."

"I can understand that."

"Well, then, I'll confess the rest," she said. "That Hanukah, in the snow outside the shul on Lessnaya Street, where Papa had a seat by the eastern wall, I realized that a bunch of yeshiva boys were staring at me. As soon as I looked up, they turned away; all except one—the oldest—who clapped his hands over his eyes. I was proud of that, too. I wanted to arouse them, make them have evil thoughts, deny God, worship me instead, like the Golden Calf. And that wasn't all."

"Tell me."

"It was still snowing a little; a few fat, wet flakes.

I caught one on my tongue and in that instant—the time it took to melt—I imagined myself in the anteroom of the shul, by the barrel filled with torn pages from the holy books, where I stripped off my coat, my dress, my woolen stockings, and my shoes. Then I ran down the aisle, between the benches, and with my arms above my head, tossing my hair, I danced naked in front of the Holy Ark and the menorah.

"That yeshiva boy—the one who'd covered up his eyes—crawled toward me on his hands and knees. He had the handle of a whip between his teeth—one with lead tips. A *nagaika.* The kind the Cossacks use. I said, 'Give it to me,' out loud, and Papa asked, 'What?' There was an icicle dangling from his mustache, under his nose.

"We went inside. Mama and I sat in the balcony, with the other women behind the linen curtain. During the prayer 'Al Hanissim,' I stuck my fist in my mouth and bit it, as hard as I could, to keep from screaming. Almighty God, I knew, who in the old days had destroyed the idolators for defiling the Holy of Holies in Jerusalem, was now going to revenge himself on me.

"I had a vision, as plain as day, of Papa on his deathbed, wearing a shroud. His eyes were closed. There were two candles stuck in brass candlesticks burning by his head. A fly on his lower lip rubbed its back legs together—I saw that vividly—and it was all my fault. That was God's revenge. It would only be a matter of time."

In the river, a three-masted schooner with one sail was heading north. The gilt figurehead on the prow glinted in the sun when it emerged from the shadow of the bridge.

Mrs. Tauber said, "This always reminds me a little of Odessa," and I followed her on the rotten planks, between the barrels and the crates, to the end of the pier, where I asked, "What happened then?"

"I got sick," she said. "For one thing, I couldn't sleep—not more than an hour or two a night, and I couldn't hold down my food, except for groats boiled in milk. I lived on that for months. Mama gave me enemas twice, sometimes three times a week; she used a calf's bladder and a goose quill."

"So did mine."

"Papa prayed and gave as much as he could to charity. One evening he tried to dose me with tea and raspberry syrup, but I became hysterical when I saw him. After all, I knew that it was either his life or mine.

"I decided to kill myself. But how? That was the question. With a kitchen knife? By drinking a glass of lye? Mama used a lot of lye to make soap. I couldn't make up my mind. The doctor, of course, was useless. A week or so after Pesach, he gave me up. I heard him say to Mama outside my door, 'She's dying.'

"I said to myself, 'God be praised.' But before I knew it, it was the middle of summer and Papa, who was frantic, shipped Mama and me off to stay with his younger sister, Sipra, who lived in a tiny village, called Raiskov, near Pereichen. 'The change will do her good,' he said. 'You'll see.'

"At first I refused to leave Sipra's house. There was a well across the road which belonged to a Russian, and I was afraid that I'd jump in it. So I stayed in bed, with my face to the wall. There were rags stuffed in the cracks between the logs."

"Yes," I said. "We did the same thing."

"Really? Did they do any good in the winter?"

"No. The wind came right through."

"That's what I figured," she said. "In any case, I lay there, like that, for almost a week. Six days, to be exact. On the morning of the seventh, I was left alone. The women went shopping; it was a Thursday, market day. I got up, put on my shoes, and ran outside. I don't know why. And I kept running. First, on the road away from town and that well. And after that, through a field of sunflowers, on my left, until I came to an orchard where four or five peasant girls with bare feet were picking up apples from the ground. They were shriveled and brown."

"That's the way peasants like to eat them."

"Yes," she said. "I know. They collected them in their torn linen skirts, which they held up with one hand, above their knees. I watched them from behind a tree and tried to make out what they were saying—my Russian is fairly good—but one of them, who had a faded blue kerchief over her head, spotted me right away.

"She straightened up and smiled. I smiled back. Then she held up the shriveled apple in her hand and said, *'Kushai. Vkusno. Ot Siroi Materi Zemli. Ponimaesh?'*

"It took me a second to figure it out. 'Eat it,' she'd said. 'It's good. From our Moist Mother Earth. You understand?' I nodded.

" 'Yes,' I said. 'I understand.'

" 'Then, eat,' she repeated, and I walked over and took a bite out of it from her hand. She burst out laughing. I laughed, too, with a mouthful.

"The breeze—it was very warm—rustled the leaves above my head. I looked up. There was an apple hanging from the end of the branch. It was yellowish-red. I thought, When it's ripe, like the others, it'll drop to the ground and rot so that next summer another can grow in its place.

"A gnat stung me on the neck. The air was filled with them. I kept waving them away from my eyes, and I noticed that, just to the right of the Russian girl, near her naked foot, there was a toad on a flat white rock.

"Why, it's the same for all of us, I thought. Every living thing. Death isn't a punishment. It's what has to be. I was flabbergasted; that had never occurred to me before. I waved the gnats away. Another one stung me on the back of the hand. The toad jumped off the rock. And then I wondered, What does God have to do with all of this? Why, nothing, I thought. He has nothing to do with the way things really are. There is no God.

"My eyes filled with tears. The girl said something else to me, but I couldn't understand. I shook my head. She let go of the ragged hem of her skirt and her apples fell to the ground. Then she threw her arms around my neck and kissed the tear from my right cheek."

We got home about one. Ostrovsky was on the stoop. He put down the *Forward*—a page of sepia photogravures—and said, "She's back. Hannele's back. She's come back with a man."

4

"WHAT MAN?" Mrs. Tauber asked. "Who is he?"

"I don't know," Ostrovsky said. "All I know is that they've been here for almost an hour. They're upstairs now. I was sitting here, reading my paper, when they came. Hannele looked right through me, like a pane of glass. Not so much as a 'Good Shabbes' out of her; nothing."

"What's he look like?" I asked.

"Tall, well-built. He wears those glasses without earpieces. You know the kind I mean? Clipped to his nose with a spring."

"Pince-nez," Mrs. Tauber said.

"Right. Pince-nez," Ostrovsky repeated. "But he's young."

He followed us into the hallway, which smelled of boiled cabbage. In the apartment on the other side of the stairs, a bed creaked and creaked and someone moaned.

"He's a Russian, too," Ostrovsky said. "But from where, exactly, I'm not sure. I can't place the accent."

"Is the old man with them?" Mrs. Tauber asked, and Ostrovsky nodded.

"God knows what he thinks," he said.

Some pot roast and two candied carrots were left over from the night before. After we ate, Mrs. Tauber took a nap. I sat for hours by the door. Twice, I started to go get Schlifka right away. What nagged me, though, was the possibility that they'd take off while I was gone. Then where would I be? I made up my mind to wait. To be on the safe side, I had to find out where they lived. At three or so, in the hallway, the printer's wife suddenly shouted, "Half a truth is a whole lie."

Apart from that, it was very quiet. It made me think of the *menukkas Shabbes*—the peace of the Sabbath—when I was a kid in Umersk. I saw myself on the dirt floor, under the table, playing knucklebones. Papa was snoozing with a handkerchief over his face. Mama went, "Shhh!" I couldn't remember what she looked like any more.

I was awakened by another loud voice from the hallway. A man said, "Don't worry. We'll be here for a while," and I opened the door a crack.

Old man Isaacs, as he passed, had a green tallis bag under his arm. He was off to shul for the evening service. Then, for a second, I saw Hannele's face in profile. The only thing I noticed, because she blinked, was the mole on her right eyelid. In the last couple of weeks, whenever I thought of her, I pictured her long black hair, but never that mole; it'd slipped my mind.

She said, "Let's wait on the stoop," and a second afterward I had a look at the man behind her, heading for the stairs. He was wearing dirty yellow spats.

I waited a while before I went after them. They were a little way up the block, at the curb, outside the kosher butcher shop. Feibush was with them. Over one shoulder he was carrying the gunny sack in which he kept his hammer and saw. The sun had already set behind the buildings across the street. The butcher, wearing a bloodstained apron, was back at work. He was standing in his doorway plucking the feathers from a chicken he held by the legs. I walked by, very slowly, in the gutter, just as Hannele said to Feibush, "But it's no trouble. Ask Roman Osipovich."

"It's no trouble at all," Roman Osipovich said.

"He's in a village called Ust Kut," Feibush said. "Have you ever heard of it?"

"It's on the Lena."

"That's the place."

"I know it very well," Roman Osipovich said. "I was exiled there myself, for two months in the winter of 1907, before they sent me to Verkholensk."

"Really? You don't say so."

"You write the letter," Roman Osipovich told him. "Don't worry about the censors. My comrades will see that he gets it."

The feathers swirled in the air. It was getting dark. The street lamp on the corner began to sizzle, and the ground-glass globe turned pink and then bright orange. The one on Canal Street, in front of Meyer's, went from violet to yellow. By that time, the three of them were sitting on the stoop, and I walked back.

"I read all your articles in the paper," Feibush was saying. "They're very good."

"You read *Die Wahrheit?*" Roman Osipovich asked him. "How come? Are you a socialist, too?"

"No, I don't know. At least, I don't think so," Feibush said.

"Then what are you?"

"What do I look like?"

"A poor Jew."

"That's what I am," Feibush said.

"That can't be all. You're too intelligent for that," Roman Osipovich said. "And what about your brother in Ust Kut?"

"To tell you the truth, we never got along very well."

Hannele yawned. Behind her, in the doorway, Tofetsky the printer had his little boy by the hand. Tofetsky's forehead was greasy with sweat.

He said, "I wonder if I could speak with you for a minute, Reb Feibush," in his thick Gallitzianer accent. Feibush looked up at him in surprise.

"Sure," he said. "Why not?"

"Just a few words, in private, if you don't mind."

"Why should I mind?"

They spoke in the hallway, behind the closed door. The little boy was left alone on the top step. He sucked the thumb of one hand and played with himself with the other.

Hannele said to me, "How are you, Jake?"

"Pretty good. And you?"

"Fine, thank you, Jake. I want you to meet a friend of mine. No . . ." She smiled dimly. "A comrade. This is Roman Osipovich Kagan. He's from Petersburg."

"How do you do," I said.

"How are you, Jake?" he asked, extending his hand. Leaning forward made his pince-nez tremble on the bridge of his nose. The round lenses reflected the light from the window on his right.

"How long have you been in America?" I asked.

"Not very long."

The door opened. Tofetsky called out, "Motele, come upstairs," and the kid disappeared.

Feibush waited a moment or two longer before he said in a low voice, "Can you beat that? He asked me for a couple of bucks. I don't get it. Is he out of work?"

"Did you give it to him?" Hannele asked.

"I gave him one. It's all I can afford. What's the matter with him? Did he lose his job?"

"He must be short," Hannele said. "He sends a money order every week, for two dollars, through Jarmulowsky's bank, to his daughter in Hamburg."

"I didn't know he had a daughter."

"Didn't he tell you the story? She's stuck in Hamburg until he can scrape up the money for her boat ticket. He only had enough for three."

"He didn't tell me that," Feibush said. "How old is she?"

"I'm not sure," Hannele said. "Thirteen, I think. She's been waiting there now for almost six months. She lives on what he sends her in a boardinghouse near the docks."

"Is that so? We stayed in one of those overnight,"

I said. "On Grosse Elbstrasse, I remember. It was as bad as the control station in Myslowice. Maybe worse. There were steam heat and electric lights, all right, but the walls were crawling with lice. It was expensive, too. A bowl of potato soup for supper cost thirty-five pfennig. We couldn't afford any. I was starved. That's some city, though. I never saw anything like it. Next to the electric trolleys, you know what impressed me the most? All those workers at dawn, with peaked caps, who swept up the streets. I couldn't believe it. You could eat off the cobblestones; they were that clean."

A minute later the old man was there. The three of them traipsed upstairs. Feibush picked up his gunny sack, from which the handle of the saw stuck out, and went down to the basement, where he rented a cot in the alcove of the Rosens' three-room apartment.

Between three and four in the morning, as far as I could judge, Mrs. Tauber's voice woke me up.

"I know the one. He's got red hair," she said in the kitchen. "Oh, that shit. That bastard."

Her voice shook. I was glad I hadn't tipped Schlifka off that afternoon. If he'd come back here to the house, Mrs. Tauber might have put two and two together about me.

I got out of bed and stood in the dark by the warped door, which was always ajar. The samovar whistled; Hannele said, "Yes," in a hoarse voice.

She went on: The rain on Canal Street had turned to sleet. Schlifka bought her a cup of coffee and they reminisced about Kiev: the Lubyankovka cemetery, with its mausoleum, under which a famous wonder-working rabbi is buried—I missed his name—and Bibikovsky Boulevard, in the spring, when the side-walks under the chestnut trees are covered with caterpillars as far as something called the Kresh-chatik.

He asked if he could see her again. "Yes," she said. "Why not?"

They met every Thursday afternoon at five-thirty, in front of the bank, after she delivered those plumes to the subcontractor next door.

"I knew what he was," she said. "Make no mistake about that. Bleiberg, my boss, saw us through the window and told me all about him the second week. He got his start in New York as a lookout, what they call a lighthouse, for a Chinese pimp on Mott Street, did you know that? They kidnapped homeless kids—boys and girls—off the street and doped them up on opium. Schlifka finally killed him, over a Polish shiksa who was twelve years old. It's common knowledge, but the cops couldn't prove anything. And that isn't all. In some ways, that's the least of it. Still, I didn't care. I looked forward to seeing him every week. I counted the days. God knows what he saw in me. My eyelids were all swollen; filled with pus. They stuck together in the morning. Do you remember that?"

"You're a very pretty girl."

"No," Hannele said. "There was something else. And he sensed it."

He bought her a phosphate, with vanilla ice cream, at Brummell's on East Twenty-third Street. And the following week he took her, by cab, to Silsbee's on Sixth Avenue, where he insisted that she try the oysters, which she loved in spite of herself. She ate a dozen of them—the first trayf she ever had—and they also drank half a bottle of non-kosher white wine. On the street, for the first time, he put his arm around her shoulders. But that was all.

Then, toward the end of February, in the cab coming home from some fancy restaurant on West Street —I think it was Garrett's—he kissed the mole on her right eyelid and, while her eyes were shut, began unbuttoning her shirtwaist at the neck.

"No," she said. "Don't. Not now."

"When?"

"Next Tuesday, I promise."

"You swear?"

"Yes, I swear," she said.

But she didn't show. She stopped work. She stayed in her apartment for a month and a half—that was when her old man took the job with the Podol Burial Society—but she couldn't stop thinking about Schlifka: his diamond ring, the thick red hair on the back of his hands. His hands frightened her. The weather got warm.

She said, "I couldn't sleep. My eyes got puffy again."

Then she began to whisper. For a few minutes I couldn't hear what she said. Finally, Mrs. Tauber repeated, "That shit," in a loud voice.

"No, it was my fault," Hannele said. "I went there of my own free will."

"But why?"

"I found that out," Hannele said.

She went one night in June to the two-room apartment on the second floor on Allen Street, where Schlifka was waiting for her in the bedroom. It had one of those big iron beds finished in white enamel, a dresser, and a chamber pot.

"Come in," he said. "Make yourself at home," and locked the door behind her. He slipped the key in his pocket. "Well? What're you waiting for?" he asked. "Take off your things."

"Turn around."

"Sure," he told her. "Whatever you say."

She unbuttoned her shirtwaist, took it off, and hung it over the bedpost. She had nothing on underneath.

"Can I look now?" he asked.

"If you like. No, wait just a second."

"What's the trouble?"

"All of a sudden, I got scared," she told Mrs. Tauber. "I was terrified that he'd hurt me. Then I got this crazy idea that, once he saw my breasts, everything would be okay. Don't ask me why, but I was convinced of it. He'd be gentle with me. I held them up in my hands and said, 'Look.'

"He turned around. 'Nice,' he said. 'Just right.'

" 'Not too small?'

" 'I've got small hands,' he said. He unbuttoned his fly, then his underpants, and took out . . . You understand what I mean. How I stared. My nipples got hard. Then he took one step forward, reached out his hand, and pinched my right nipple between his thumb and forefinger. I screamed. He grabbed me by the throat, pulled me toward him, and threw me sideways on the bed. I tried to get up, but he slapped me twice very hard across the face with his left hand, the one with the ring. I screamed again and rolled over on the mattress.

"There was no sheet, just a filthy woolen blanket that smelled from vomit. I tried to cover myself up with it. He yanked it away and ripped off my skirt, my drawers—they were very pretty, my best, cambric trimmed with lace—and pulled off my shoes, one after the other. I heard them drop on the floor. I wasn't wearing any stockings. Then he took my shirtwaist off the bedpost and ripped that, too, with one hand and his teeth."

He kept her locked up in that room, naked, for a week and a half, shtupping her—her own word—again and again.

"And not only in the right place," she said.

She paused. "He fed me mostly on lentil soup," she said. "Which he cooked himself on the stove in the kitchen. I suppose that's all he could manage. God knows, it's cheap. But he liked it, too. Sometimes we ate together from the same saucepan, with the same wooden spoon. There was also salt pork in it. Little pieces; he told me so. But I didn't care. I was never hungry.

"He made me drink at least half a glass of bourbon a day. There must have been something in it. It nauseated me. I couldn't keep my eyes open. Half the time I didn't know where I was. When the trains roared by on the El, the whole place shook. The window rattled. That always brought me around a little.

"One time I heard a woman's voice in the room. I was under that itchy blanket, sweltering. Schlifka covered me with it. I didn't have the strength . . . I couldn't lift a finger . . . to throw it off.

"The woman said, 'Let's have a look,' and stripped me. I managed to open my eyes. She was fat, with dyed blond hair. When she leaned over me, I saw the black roots.

"She poked her finger into everything, everywhere, and then smelled it. Even in my ears, I swear. She sniffed the wax stuck under her fingernail from my ears. Then she felt me all over. She ran her dry, hot hands all over me. That, somehow, was the worst, that woman touching me."

She paused again. "No," she said. "That's not true. The worst, the very worst, was later—I don't know when—after he stopped drugging me. He wanted me awake, you see, so I'd know what was happening. That's what he said.

"One night I came around; I had an awful headache. He was beside the bed. I sat up. He grabbed me by the hair and slapped my face. He wouldn't let go. He forced my head back and pinched the inside of my thighs, one after the other, with his left hand. Then he shtupped me. After that, he went into the kitchen and came back with a basin of water and a piece of soft red flannel.

" 'Don't move,' he said. I lay there with my eyes shut. He washed off my face with the wet rag; then my whole body, all over, very gently, like I was a baby. Just with water, though; no soap. He says soap gives him a rash.

"The room was so hot I dried off right away, until I started sweating again. And then, after that, with my head in his naked lap, he combed out my tangled hair. With a tortoise-shell comb, like the one I have at home.

"The next night he did it again . . . everything . . . and the night after that. Night after night after night. My thighs were all black and blue—yellow, too. I couldn't stand the touch of that rag on them. So you know what he did? Squeezed a little water from the flannel; it felt good.

"No," she said. "It excited me, and he knew it. I begged him, 'Please,' and he'd shtup me again, but always here, up the backside, where it hurt, and never gave me any pleasure at all. At least not until . . . One night he caught me . . . you know . . . trying, with my finger, to . . . You understand what I mean? I'd never done such a thing before. He hit me so hard I fell on the floor. 'Only I poke something in there,' he said. 'Me. Get it?' He said if I ever touched myself again, he'd break my finger. And he meant it. I saw it in those blue eyes. 'Yes,' I said, and when I obeyed him the next night, he did what I wanted and I fainted from the joy. Not for long; two or three seconds, just after he . . . when I felt the gush inside me. Afterward I . . . That was the worst, the very worst, by far."

One night he brought her a new dress—one made out of fine red percale, with two box pleats down the back—but no underwear—and told her, "Put it on."

"We went for a walk on Allen Street," she said. "Two or three blocks. And I held his hand. Can you imagine that? I reached for it going down the stairs. The next night he handed me a nickel and let me go out alone. I walked as far as Houston Street, where I bought a bag of sunflower seeds—I love salted sunflower seeds—and turned around and came back to him.

" 'Good girl,' he said to me in English. 'Very good'; and I was so happy to have pleased him that I grabbed his hand again and kissed it; the same one, the left, with the diamond ring.

"The next night, when he let me go out alone again, I ran away. I was afraid to come back here, where he'd find me, but I didn't know what else to do. I had no money, either; I'd given the nickel to a beggar on the corner. He had no nose. He frightened me. I don't know why.

"It was very hot. The next thing I knew, I was on East Broadway, outside the Café Neva. My throat was parched. I went inside and asked the waiter for a glass of water. Roman Osipovich was at a table near the window, drinking a glass of tea. That's what I really wanted: a glass of hot tea. I stared at him. He looked up from the book he was reading—something in Russian—and said, 'Are you all right?' That's how we met. He knows almost everything. I blurted it out, that night in the café, eating chick peas from a plate and drinking tea."

Someone scraped a chair across the kitchen floor. Mrs. Tauber said nothing. I heard a click. It took me a second to realize it was the latch on the front door. Hannele was gone.

I was asleep on my feet, light-headed, with gritty eyes, and loose bowels as well. I had to go to the can in the hallway before I could follow Hannele and Roman Osipovich downstairs. I caught up with them on the stoop, along with Feibush, who said, "It's harder than I thought, after all this time. I worked on it all night, but it's still not right. Can I bring it to you when I'm finished?"

"It's better that I pick it up here," Roman Osipovich said.

"Whatever you say."

"I've got an article to finish," he said. "What about tonight between twelve and one?"

"That's fine with me."

"Good. We'll see you then."

"I appreciate it," Feibush said. "Thanks."

"For what? *Nichevo,*" he said in Russian. "It's nothing."

They shook hands. "By the way," Roman Osipovich asked. "What's your brother's first name?"

"Mordechai."

"Is that the name he uses over there?"

"I don't know."

"Well, no matter, Ust Kut is a tiny place. My comrades will find him."

"There's something else you ought to know about him," Feibush said.

"What's that?"

"He's not a Social Democrat."

"What is he?"

"A Social Revolutionary."

"What's the difference?" I asked.

Roman Osipovich took off his pince-nez and rubbed it on his sleeve. He said, "The little jug has big ears."

"I was standing right here," I said. "I couldn't help overhearing."

The spring left red marks on either side of the

bridge of his nose; his eyes looked smaller. They were a yellow-brown.

"Will you do it?" Feibush asked him.

"Is he Left or Right?"

"Left."

"Yes," Roman Osipovich said. "I give you my word. It'll be done." He clipped the glasses back on and stared at me. "Why do you want to know about such things?" he asked.

"I'm interested."

"Why?"

"I've got my reasons."

"What are they?"

"What's it to you?"

"Leave the kid alone," Hannele said. "He's okay."

"Is he?"

"Were you in Petersburg in 1905?" I asked.

"Yes," he said. "I was there."

"Did you kill any Cossacks?"

"No."

"That's too bad."

He smiled. "There were more important things to do."

"Like what?"

"I was a delegate to the Soviet."

"What's that?"

"That was an elected organization of workers," he said. "The first one in history."

"Are you a worker?"

"Full-time," he said.

"What do you do?"

"I help move history along."

"How do you do that?"

"In a lot of ways," he said. "Sometime, maybe, we'll talk about it."

"Anytime you say."

"Maybe tonight."

He took Hannele by the hand. They walked north toward Stanton Street for three blocks, which was a lucky break for me. It was my direction to get to work; I could follow them without arousing any suspicion. All I had to do was keep them in sight. That was easy, in spite of the crowds, because Hannele was still wearing her red dress, the one with the two box pleats down the back. I could see her half a block away. On Broome Street, though, they made a right. I ran like hell, and just as I turned the corner I saw them cross the street in front of the livery stable and go into a building.

There was a Cheap Charlie on the ground floor: a candy store where Papa once bought me a bag of chocolate-covered walnuts for Purim. I ducked down behind a pushcart. It was my lucky day. Between the spokes of the wheel, I saw Roman Osipovich turn around and give the street the once-over before he went through the open door.

5

AFTER WORK, my stomach was still on the blink. I drank a glass of tea with lemon in a café on Ludlow Street, then walked to Allen, and headed downtown to the whorehouse. Just outside, a train slowing down for the Rivington Street station sent a shower of blue sparks through the air. The cobbler on the third floor sat in his open doorway. This time, the candle flickering on the workbench between his legs gleamed on an awl in his hand. He had a wart on the side of his nose.

Yetta knew me right away. She said in Yiddish, "Red told me all about you. He'll be back in a little while. Come in and make yourself at home."

The parlor was empty. It stank from cheap perfume, dust, disinfectant, and stale tobacco. Those burlap sacks were nailed to the floor. I sat on the wooden bench. The ceiling was very low. The fringed shade on the window was drawn. On the table in the opposite corner, to my right, was a pink banquet lamp decorated with red roses and green leaves. The wick made a sucking noise; it was turned way down.

"Care for something to drink?" Yetta asked me.

"No, I don't think so, thanks."

A door down the hall opened and slammed shut. A girl with a Litvak accent yelled in Yiddish, "Is that Red?"

Even before I laid eyes on her, from the tone of her voice I knew she was the one hooked on morphine. She came into the light. Her skin was yellow. She had dark-brown eyes; the left pupil was much bigger than the right. The door down the hall opened again, a man called out, "Hey, Rosa," and she turned around again.

"Let me know as soon as Red gets here," she said.

"One of these days Red is going to murder that cunt," Yetta said.

She used the English word; I'd never heard a woman do that before. I stared at her dyed blond hair, with the black roots, her long red fingernails, the gold ring on her pinky, and the necklace of blue stones set in silver around her fat neck.

"Anything wrong?" she asked.

"Not at all."

She took a swig from a bottle of rye on the table. "Sure you won't have some?"

I shook my head. There was a knock on the door

and she answered it. Something clinked; I thought it was the necklace until I realized it came from the pocket of her kimono. A little guy in a straw hat came into the room; he wore a pointed goatee streaked with gray. They whispered together in Yiddish until I heard her say, "For you, Reb Schneider, anything."

"How much?"

"Two bucks."

She took his money and yelled, "Sophie, get your ass in here."

A girl ran in; her taffeta petticoat rustled. She was the one with the scaly rash on the nape of her neck. She also had it bad on the inside of her forearm, near the elbow. I saw that patch in the lamplight; she reached for a brass token, about the size of half a buck, that Yetta took from her pocket.

"What's that for?" I asked.

She clinked the others together in her pocket. "That's the way I keep count," she said, sitting beside me. "What about you? Here for some fun?"

"I'm here to see Schlifka."

"Yes, of course," she said. "Hannele."

"That's right."

"He's got the hots for that girl," she said. "But bad. I knew he would. He goes for that type in a big way."

"Which type is that?"

"Well, for one thing, her papa's a rabbi. And deep down, she believes, too. It's in her blood. Red's got a soft spot for pious Jewish girls." She laughed. "Don't ask me why. It's been that way for as long as I can remember."

"How long is that?"

"A long time. I've known him since he was a kid, two or three years older than you, working as a lighthouse for a Chink on Mott Street."

"I've heard about that."

"I had my eye on him for months. When he got into trouble and went on the lam, I took him in for six months—I had a nice two-room apartment on Henry Street—until the trouble blew over. Him and that Polish shiksa."

"What happened to her?"

"Wanda? He had to get rid of her. She came at him one day in the kitchen with a butcher knife, so he broke her nose—like this, with the side of his hand—and threw her out on her ass."

"Why?"

"She was jealous of me. Don't laugh. I was younger then, and good-looking, too. Thin. But most important of all, I've got a good head for business. And that's what counts, believe me. Red knew it. We've been together ever since."

Another train roared by, right beneath the window. The shade flapped against the pane, the chimney rattled in the lamp, and the bottle of rye on the edge of the table fell on the floor.

"No harm done," Yetta said, picking it up, pulling the cork out with her teeth, spitting it out, and taking another swig.

The little guy with the straw hat left. A different girl walked into the room. She was the best-looking one yet; a blonde, with straight hair that reached her shoulders, and blue eyes. She was wearing a corset cover with an embroidered V neck. One of the straps, trimmed with lace, had slipped off her shoulder, down her arm.

The guy who'd obviously been with Rosa stalked in, buttoning up his black sateen shirt. "That broad ain't worth shit," he said in English, just as Schlifka opened the front door.

"Which broad?" he asked.

"Rosa," the guy said. "I want my money back."

"What's the matter with her?"

"She's sick," he said. "She's in there gagging now."

"Here, give her two of these," Schlifka said to Yetta in Yiddish. "But only two. Keep the bottle."

"I want my money back," the guy repeated.

"I'll give you this up your ass," Schlifka said, holding up his walking stick. The guy left.

Schlifka yelled down the hall in Yiddish again, "Tell her I'll be there in a minute," and then he spotted me.

"Don't get up," he said. "Stay where you are. It's good to see you."

The blonde grinned—she had a space between her front teeth—and whispered to me in English, "He's got a load on."

"How can you tell?"

"He's got that look in his eye," she said.

"What look is that?"

"Just watch yourself," she whispered.

He sat down beside me and said, "Tell me the good news."

"Hannele's back."

"With another guy?"

"Some Russian, by the name of Kagan."

"Kagan?" he repeated. "I don't know no cadet who's a Russian by the name of Kagan."

"What's a cadet?"

"A pimp," the blonde said. "It's a fancy name for a pimp."

"No, he's no pimp," I said.

"Then what is he?" Schlifka asked.

"He says he's a worker, but he wears whatchamacallits—those things you button over your shoes."

"Spats?" Schlifka said.

"Is that the English? He also writes articles for some paper."

"Which one, do you know?"

"Die Wahrheit," I said.

"You're kidding." He laughed. "That beats everything. What do you know about that?" He licked the ends of three fingers, smoothed down his shiny hair, up front, on either side of the part, and asked, "Where are they now?"

"At his place."

"Where's that?"

"Where they're safe," I said. "Until you cough up another five bucks for me."

"What's this? We had a deal. I thought we was pals."

"Business is business; you know how it is."

"I like you," he said. "Tell you what I'll do. I'll give you three bucks plus any pussy you want in the house; and for as long as you want it, free. What do you say to that?"

"I don't know."

"What's the matter? Don't you go for pussy?"

"Sure I do."

"But you never had one, is that it?"
"That's got nothing to do with it."
"Admit it," he said. "You're scared."
"No, I ain't."
"Then take your pick. What about Judy over here? Don't you like her?"
"She's okay."
"She'll do whatever you want," he said.
"I want the five bucks."
"Are you nuts? Just look at her; those tits. She's a shiksa, from Corning, New York. A farm girl. Fresh as a daisy."
"That's me," Judy said. "A little wildflower from a farm right outside Corning. Plucked, but still fresh, like Red says. Want a smell?"
Schlifka laughed again. "Ain't that the kind of girl you dream about?" he said. "A piece like that? Tell me the truth."
"Yes."
"You play with yourself a lot, don't you?"
"No," I said. "Never."
"Don't kid me. Look at them pimples on your chin." He propped his walking stick up against the bench beside him. "What does she do in your dreams? You can tell me."
"A lot of things."
"Like what? Does she put her hand between your thighs, like this?"
"Yes."
"And give you a squeeze?"
"Don't," I said.
"What else?" he asked. "Does she kiss you?"
"Yes."

"How?"
"All kinds of ways."
He grabbed the back of my neck with his right hand.
"Let go," I said.
"Does she do it like this?" he asked. His breath stank from bourbon and cigars. "Tell me," he said. "With her tongue between your lips? In your mouth? Like this?"
I shoved him away with both hands. His eyes were shut, his tongue out.
"What about my five bucks?"
"First tell me where they are."
"On Broome Street, between Orchard and Ludlow," I said. "I don't know the number. But it's right across from the livery stable, and there's a Cheap Charlie on the ground floor."
"Good enough," he said. "Here's the five bucks. You earned it."
The girl took me by the hand. "Come on," she said. "How about it?"
I stood up. "Sure. What the hell? Why not?"
"Atta way."
Schlifka called out down the hall in Yiddish, "Mama, come in here."
"You want Rosa?" Yetta yelled back.
"I want you," he said. "Now."
We passed her going down the hall.
I heard Schlifka behind me say, "Take off your clothes."
"Let's go to my room."
"No, take off the kimono," he said. "Everything.

The necklace, too, and that ring. That's it. Now walk around."

In the room at the end of the hallway, the girl closed the door, turned up the gas, and said, "How old are you, anyway?"

"Eighteen."

"You don't look it," she said. "You don't feel it, either."

"Don't do that."

"Tell me the truth," she said. "Do you shave?"

"No."

"I didn't think so. Well, that ain't nothing to be ashamed of."

"How old are you?" I asked her.

"How old do I look?"

"Eighteen, too."

"I'll be twenty in January."

"You sure don't look it. It must be because you grew up on a farm."

"Don't kid yourself. That's ball-breaking work. That's why I come to New York," she said. "This here is a snap in comparison."

"You don't say."

"I do," she said. "I had to get up at three-thirty every morning to milk the cows. We had pigs, too. I fed them slops. In the fall, I had to scrape off the bristles after they was butchered and scalded. Do you know anything about pigs?"

"Not much."

"We had a sow once that gobbled up her babies alive. It was horrible. I love it here. I can get up at four in the afternoon, if I want."

"I see what you mean."

"Why don't you sit down on the bed and I'll take off your clothes."

"I can do that myself."

"Come on, relax," she said, unbuttoning my shirt. "Do you have to take a leak? There's a chamber pot under the bed."

"No, I don't think so," I said. "But maybe a crap. Do you mind?"

"I'll wait outside."

"I'd appreciate it," I said. "Have you got any paper?"

"Just a copy of *The Police Gazette.*"

"That'll do fine."

Five minutes later she knocked at the door, and I said, "Come in. It was only gas."

"That's nerves," she said.

"I guess so."

"It's only natural."

"It's hot in here, you know that?"

"That's nerves, too," she said. "Can I make a suggestion?"

"What's that?"

"Take off your shoes and socks."

"You're right," I said. "I forgot."

"Do you want me to open the window?"

"No, it's okay."

"Good," she said. "Now let's get down to it. Would you like to strip me?"

"No, you do it."

"How's that?"

"Very nice," I said. "Now the petticoat."

"I'm getting fat around the middle. It's all that

Jewish cooking in this joint; the blintzes and sour cream."

"No, you're just right," I said. "Would you do me another favor?"

"Name it."

"Lift your arms above your head."

"Like this?"

"Yeah."

"What else?"

"Nothing," I said. "Except a question."

"What's that?"

"How come your nipples are so red?"

"Rouge."

"Really?"

"That's Mama's idea. She makes all her girls use it. She lines us up, as naked as jay birds, in the parlor, and smears it on us herself every afternoon just before we open up. Nothing on the face, though, not even lipstick. She don't allow it. 'It's cheap,' she says. 'But on the tits is class.' Do you like it?"

"Very much. What're you doing?"

"What do you think? I'm getting in bed. Move over. No, silly, not all the way over there. Snuggle up. That's better. Say, you're wringing wet, you know that?"

"It's hot in here."

"Just take it easy," she said. "Relax."

"I'm trying."

"Take a couple of deep breaths. No, not so fast. You'll get dizzy."

"I'm okay now."

"Then get on top of me," she said. "But gentle. Watch them elbows. Very good."

"Now what?"

"Whatever you want. Don't you like my tits?"

"I think they're beautiful."

"Then give them a feel," she said. "Wait, it's easier if we roll over."

"Which way?"

"It makes no difference. Roll off and lay down on your right side. That's it. Now use your left hand. How's that?"

"Very nice."

"Use your mouth, too. Don't be afraid. Suck. Do what you like. Just don't bite. That's the way. Now the other one. What's the matter?"

"It ain't doing any good."

"Keep sucking and spread your legs. Say, that's real nice. You're well hung, too."

"It's no use," I said. "I can't get it up."

"Don't get yourself into a sweat. That's the way it happens sometimes. It's nothing to worry about. We'll try something else. Roll over on your stomach. That's it. Now stick your ass up in the air."

"Like this?"

"Exactly," she said. "Now hold it. There we go."

"What's that?"

"Just my finger," she said. "How do you like it?"

"I don't."

"What's the matter?"

"Take it out," I said. "Please."

"Give it a minute. Let me wiggle it around a little."

"No, take it out," I repeated. "Please. I'm scared I'll crap."

"Where you going?"

"To get dressed," I said. "I don't think this is going to work."

"Don't be silly. Come and lay down."

"Where did I put my other sock?"

"Do like I tell you," she said. "Lay down on your back."

"Maybe for a minute."

"Atta boy."

"What're you doing?"

"What's the matter? Does my twat smell?"

"Not a bit," I said. "No."

"Go ahead and lick it, if you want."

"No, thank you."

"Then lay still and spread your legs wider."

"Like this?"

"Perfect."

"That feels good," I told her. "That's terrific. Oh, yeah, that's it. Keep it up. That's wonderful."

"You see? It's stiff."

"Don't talk. Use your tongue again. More." Then I yelled, "Hold it, hold it. Oh, my God."

She spit into the enameled basin on the washstand in the corner and then rinsed out her mouth from the pitcher.

"I'll have you know that's something special," she said. "I don't do that for nobody except Red."

"I'm sorry," I told her. "I really am. I appreciate it."

"What's that?"

"Five bucks," I said. "Take it, please."

"I can't do that. You're Red's pal. He'd kill me if I took a dime from you."

"He don't have to find out."

"He knows everything that goes on around here. Anyway, we're not allowed to handle any cash at all. Just these," she said, scooping up a handful of those brass tokens from the washstand.

"I got one more favor to ask you," I said. "The most important."

"What is it now?"

"Don't tell Schlifka?"

"About what?"

"That I had trouble getting it up."

"That's between you, me, and the bedpost," she said. "I swear."

The walking stick was propped against the bench between Schlifka's thighs. "It ain't all it's cracked up to be, is it?" he said.

"It's okay."

"No, for guys like us, there are better things. Higher things." He switched to Yiddish. "Spiritual things."

"Spiritual things?"

He rambled on in Yiddish. The words were occasionally slurred. Now and again he took a nip from his own quart: Kentucky bourbon in a brown bottle. His hand shook; the glass clicked against his front teeth.

It strikes me now that he was using Yiddish because it was the language of his childhood; that's what he talked about for over an hour. His parents died of cholera when he was eleven. He was adopted by his father's older brother, Nachman, a peddler. They tramped from town to town. The peasants nicknamed Nachman "Kyrylo Kozhymiaka" after the famous giant in the Ukrainian fairy tale who was a tanner; he could rip a stack of twelve wet hides in half with his bare hands.

"Also, in the stories, this Kyrylo Kozhymiaka has a very long beard," Schlifka said. "Well, so did Nachman. It was black. Only he wore payess, too, a yarmulke and tzitzis."

"Was he really so strong?"

"I found that out."

He and Nachman followed the west bank of the Dnieper every spring after the rains, from Kiev to the Black Sea. They peddled cheap pottery, matches, boot and axle grease, rags, and bones. At night they slept in the fields. Nachman always washed his hands —sometimes with dew from the grass—and recited the benediction before they ate their handful of warmed-up kasha; they used oak or linden leaves as plates. The boy kept the fire going. Nachman read aloud from a Yiddish translation of the Five Books of Moses he carried, wrapped in a kerchief, at the bottom of his sack.

He told stories he remembered from his own childhood: how, after death, the spirit stays on the tip of the nose until the face rots, when the angel Duma carries it off to heaven or hell. He described the dead rising from their graves at the End of Days and Messiah judging all the goyim—the sons of Esau—on Mt. Seir in the Holy Land. He said that the unrighteous among them will burn up from the heat of the sun. It'll shine day and night, all year long, with the brightness it once had in the Garden of Eden, before the Fall.

"How bright was that?" the boy asked.

"We can't imagine it."

"And will it be as hot as this?" he asked, kicking a log in the fire.

"Much hotter."

One end of the log was charred; the boy said, "That's not hot enough for me."

He prayed for the End of Days to come quickly. In the villages, the peasants sicced their dogs on them. One hot summer day, outside of Cherkassy, Nachman stuck the boy in the fork of a beech tree, turned around, and faced the dog running toward them down the road. It had yellow eyes, like a wolf; its ears were back. A tuft of reddish fur bristled on the nape of its neck.

The boy scrambled up higher, to the next branch, just as the dog jumped for Nachman's throat. He kicked it in the balls. It yelped, flipped over backward, and landed on its haunches, with its tail between its legs. Nachman kicked it again, under the jaw. It lay panting on its side in the dirt. Nachman reached down, stuck his right hand between the white teeth, and ripped out its tongue.

"We ran like hell," Schlifka said. "For five or six versts, without stopping, until we reached the next town—I forget the name. It was right on the river, though. I remember that, because Nachman spent half an hour washing the blood from his hands."

He took another drink. Yetta, from the entrance to the hallway, said, "Red, she's climbing the walls."

"Tell her to go fuck herself," he said in English. "Where was I?"

"By the river," I said.

He reverted again to Yiddish. "That's the way it

was," he said. "The whole time. Dogs, peasants . . . Sometimes they came after us with sickles. Their brats threw stones."

The bottle clicked again against his teeth. Yetta was gone. I heard Rosa scream, "I can't stand it."

Schlifka polished off the rest of the booze in one gulp and caught the last two drops on his tongue. He tossed the empty bottle away; the neck shattered against the windowsill. There was brown glass all over the floor.

He went on. "When I was thirteen, we stopped one night at an inn on a road south of Dneprodzerzhinsk, two or three versts outside of town. It was very hot. Nachman wanted a drink, a glass of vodka. Besides the innkeeper, who was Polish, I remember—he spoke with a Polish accent—the place was empty, except for a peasant at the table in front of the tile stove. The fire was out. He was drunk. About thirty, I think, maybe a little more, with straw-colored hair, high cheekbones, and slanted eyes, like a Tartar, but blue . . . very blue. There was a half-empty bottle of vodka in front of him on the table, but no glass.

"When we walked in, he had one foot up on the bench. He was wrapping a linen strip around his leg; the kind peasants wear instead of socks. We wore them, too. He also had on bast sandals, like Nachman and me. We sat down at the table by the door.

"Nachman ordered two vodkas in Russian; we both spoke Russian very well.

" 'Over my dead body, kikes,' the peasant says.

"The innkeeper didn't want any trouble. He said, 'Mikola Ivanovich, you're drunk. Go home.'

"The peasant put his foot down, without finishing

the job; the wrapping was still loose. He took a scrap of newspaper from his back pocket, tore off a strip, sprinkled a pinch of *makhorka* in it, rolled it up, licked the edge, and said to Nachman, 'Hey, kike, you got a match?'

"Nachman put his hands on the table. The innkeeper said, 'Here's a match, Mikola Ivanovich,' and put it down beside his elbow, on the edge of the table.

"Mikola Ivanovich said, 'What's the matter, kike? Are you deaf? Didn't you hear me?'

" 'I heard you,' Nachman said, looking him right in the eye.

"The goy shredded the cigarette between his fingers all over the floor. But he stuck the match between his teeth. Then, very fast, he jumped up on the table, lay down on the small of his back, and lifted up his legs. You understand what I mean? His ass was pointed at us. Then, with his left hand, he lit the match on the seat of his pants, held it up to his asshole, and farted. I heard it. It caught fire. I couldn't believe my eyes. A blue flame, a foot long, shot out of his asshole at us.

" 'That's for you,' he said. 'You Christ-killing sons of bitches. You motherfuckers. A taste of things to come.' He sat up next to the vodka bottle and dangled his legs over the table; the linen strip hung down. 'In hell,' he said. 'From the Evil One . . .' He crossed himself. 'Special for kikes.' He started wrapping the strip around his leg again. 'Do you know about that?' he said.

" 'The Evil One has a hairy asshole as wide as the doorway of holy St. Vladimir's in Kiev. And when he farts, it's like the north wind. Not here, but in Dudinka, off the taiga, in January. I did my six years in the army there, for the Little Father, may God protect him, so I know what that wind is like. It cuts you to the bone.

" 'But that's nothing in comparison to the fart. He lays there, on his scaly back, grinding up Judas between his teeth—another kike. That gives him a lot of gas, like red cabbages. Under him, and all around, for a thousand versts, are red-hot coals. All he has to do is keep his tail out of the way, lift his hairy ass a little, and let one rip. A blue flame, as long as from here to Odessa—longer—shoots out of his hairy asshole. All that hair is singed. The flame burns up all the kikes, the Christ-killers, who're jammed together up to their chins in a lake of green snot. It fries them alive, over and over again, forever.'

"He tucked in the end of the wrapping and said, 'That's Christ's truth. But you don't have to take my word for it. You'll see for yourselves. And who knows? Maybe soon.' "

The boy began to shake.

"Drink up your vodka," Nachman told him.

"I can't pick up the glass," he whispered.

"Never mind, then. Let's go." He left a ruble on the table, picked up his pack, and they went out. There was no moon; it was very dark. They headed south on the dusty road.

After a few minutes, Nachman stopped and grabbed the boy by the arm. "Shhh!" he said. "Listen."

"What is it?" the boy asked.

"Don't you hear him?"

"Who?"

"He's right behind us, up the road."

"That's the wind in the trees."

"No, it's him," Nachman said. "I'm sure of it. Listen."

Carried on the wind, which rustled the leaves, was a drunken, wavering voice.

The Holy Mother
Shines her candle
In the empty tomb . . .

It was the peasant singing. He was coming closer. Just before a bend in the road, near a big fir tree, he tripped and fell; the boy heard the thud. Then the singing began again.

Our Shepherd lives . . .

Nachman whispered, "Run."

"Where?" the boy asked.

"Straight ahead, as fast as you can, and keep going. Don't stop."

"What are you going to do?"

"Don't worry about me," Nachman said. He picked up a flat white stone from the side of the road with both hands.

The boy took off. He kept running as fast as he could, on the mound between the wagon ruts. He ran until he dropped. Then he lay there in the dirt.

"I was dizzy, sweating, out of breath," Schlifka said. "And shaking like a leaf. Finally, I raised my head. The sky was cloudy. There was no moon or stars. I could hardly see my hand in front of my face. I thought to myself, It's come. The End of Days. But with darkness, not light. It's here.

"I shut my eyes and opened them again. Nothing. All I saw was the top of another fir tree above me against the sky. It was swaying. But the earth itself was pitch-dark. And it was as if that darkness was more than just the absence of light. It was something else. I can't explain it. Then I realized that I could hear everything; not just the creaking branches, the rustling leaves . . . things like that . . . but a weasel as well, creeping through the dry grass on my left. I knew what it was. Don't ask me how. It was out hunting. There were bats, too, flitting around, along with an owl right over me, rising on the wind. It had a live mouse in its claws. I heard it squeal."

Nachman found him in a ditch on the side of the road. He was half-conscious; his mouth and one nostril were stuffed with dirt.

"I remember spitting it out and blowing my nose in my fingers," Schlifka said. "But I couldn't stand up. My knees gave way. He picked me up and tossed me over his right shoulder; on the other was the pack."

Nachman carried him over his shoulder and then on the back of his neck, sitting up, for the rest of the night and the next day until noon, when he got back the use of his legs.

"One of Nachman's sleeves, near the shoulder, was stained with dried blood," Schlifka said. "Not much. A reddish-brown blotch, about the size of your hand. But he tore the whole sleeve off and threw it away. He looked funny, with one arm bare, but I didn't mention it."

At a bend in the Dnieper, they headed west and kept going, day and night for almost two weeks. They crossed the Bazavluk in a ferry, and then the steppe, where the dry wind, blowing in their faces, carried with it the smell of scorched wheat. They finally settled in a town called Veseli, where Nachman died of typhoid fever the following spring.

"He never mentioned what happened," Schlifka said. "Not one word, even at the end, when he was delirious. I thought about it a lot. I still think about it. You want to know something? And this is the truth. Once in a while, in the dark, I still hear things."

"What kind of things?"

"There's a rat, where I live, behind the bedroom wall."

From the entrance to the hallway, Yetta said, "Red, you'd better come."

I followed him. The first door on the left was open. Rosa, on the edge of the bed, gagged into a handkerchief. A hairpin dangled on her forehead. Schlifka went into the room, bent over, and whispered in her ear.

"Yes," she said. "Please."

"First things first."

He got down on one knee and picked up the chamber pot by both handles. Then he stood up and dumped it over her head. Her mouth was open.

On my way out the front door, I bumped into a young guy wearing a yellow puff tie with a pearl stuck in it, and one of those haircloth summer hats with an upturned brim.

6

I GOT BACK to Mrs. Tauber's by ten. Hannele and Roman Osipovich were in the kitchen. He was telling Feibush about some chemist called Nikolaev, a Social Revolutionary who'd been killed by the premature explosion of a bomb he was making in his apartment near the Nevsky Prospekt in Petersburg.

"He taught me to drink tea with a slice of apple dipped in honey, instead of lemon and sugar," Roman Osipovich said. "But his sacrifice was useless." He breathed on those round lenses of his pince-nez, and rubbed them on his sleeve. "What would the assassination of Witte have accomplished? Nothing. We got Stolypin. And what good did it do to shoot him? None. Another member of the ruling class took his place. No, it's only the inexorable laws of history which will bring about the Revolution."

"What laws are those?" I asked.

Feibush, who ignored me, said, "I don't understand. If these laws exist, as you say, then what good can you do? The Revolution will happen anyway, no matter what."

"You're right," Roman Osipovich said. "It's a contradiction; at least, that's the way it seems. How can I explain it? To be a Marxist is to be at the same time a fatalist and . . . what? A midwife, so to speak. Yes. You know that the child will be born anyway, but you do what you can to help. You reach in and, with bloody hands, accelerate the process."

"That can be fatal to the baby," Mrs. Tauber said.

"It's a chance we have to take."

"And the mother?"

"Sometimes she miscarries," he said. "In 1905 the masses rebelled spontaneously and failed. To be honest, we were caught by surprise. All we did, at first, was follow their lead. But we've learned a lot since then; all of us. The masses, too. The next time, believe me, things will be very different."

"And when will that be?" Mrs. Tauber asked.

"I wish I knew. Sometimes, to be honest, I don't think I'll live to see it. Then I get the feeling that it's right around the corner; that the Revolution, the Dictatorship of the Proletariat, the establishment of the classless society, the end of History, as we know it, is almost at hand."

"Do you really believe in all of that?" Feibush asked.

"Yes, I really do. And when it happens, I believe that the human race will be transformed."

"How?" I asked.

"Who knows? Do you like music?"

"So-so," I said. "It depends."

"Can you sing?"

"A little."

"Well, I believe, for example, that our voices will become more musical, even the way we speak. Yes, I mean it," he said. "The vocal cords, our whole body will change. We'll live a hundred years or more."

"And when that happens, will kids still get run over by beer trucks?" Feibush asked.

Hannele burst out laughing.

"Beer trucks?" Roman Osipovich repeated.

Feibush put his arm around Mrs. Tauber's shoulders. "Miriam told me about a ten-year-old kid, last spring, who was run over by a beer truck on Second Avenue. A wheel crushed his head."

"I don't get it," I said. "What's that got to do with anything?"

Roman Osipovich clipped on his glasses, stared at Feibush across the table covered with a lace cloth, and said, "Yes, that's true. You have a point. There's no question about it. But you must understand this. From the perspective of history, the individual doesn't mean a damn thing; neither you nor me nor that kid with the crushed head under the wheels of that beer truck. It's the ultimate transfiguration of the masses that counts; the whole species. And accidents aside, when that happens—when man, at last, lives a just life . . . You've been around," he said to me. "You've seen people die."

"Yes," I said.

"And were they scared?"

"Yes."

"Why?"

"Why the hell do you think?"

"I'll tell you," he said. "It's not death itself, or dying, that terrifies us, but the realization at the end that our lives have been meaningless."

"Maybe so. I don't know."

"I do," he said. "Listen to me. When that time finally comes when human beings will be fulfilled, when life—the collective experience—means something, then we'll die without being afraid. We'll close our eyes, fold our hands on our chests, and wait for the end with a kind of joy. We'll accept it with serenity—the serenity that comes from having lived on this earth like gods."

"Is that the truth?"

"Yes," he told me. "That's the truth."

"You know what I believe in? It just hit me," Feibush said. "I believe in chance."

"And that's all?" Roman Osipovich asked.

"Nothing else; it's an accident—the whole thing."

"I can't live in a world like that."

Mrs. Tauber took a tin of Wisotsky tea from the shelf above the stove and pried the top off with a knife.

Feibush said, "Tell me something about Ust Kut."

"I was lucky," Roman Osipovich said. "I sat there for only one winter and the following summer, then they shipped me south."

"What was it like?"

"Cold," he said. "Very cold. The horses' breath froze on their muzzles; the peasants had to break off the icicles so they could breathe. I lived in a peasant hut, between the woods and the river. It belonged to a trapper and his wife: Old Believers. They were always drunk on homemade vodka, or something called *mesimarya;* it was red—ruby-colored—and very sweet. They brewed it from some kind of berry that was ripened by the midnight sun during the summer. Not bad, I have to admit.

"But the winter nights were terrible. The hut was alive with cockroaches, which made a rustling noise with their wings. They were everywhere: on the table, the bed, crawling on our faces when we tried to catch a little sleep. From time to time, we had to move out of the hut, which had a sod roof covered with snow, for a day or two, and leave the door wide open to get rid of them. And outside, you understand, the temperature was fifty below zero."

"And the summer?" Feibush asked.

"Worse, in a way. We were plagued by tiny black flies, clouds of them, that stung like hell. They killed a cow, I remember, that got lost in the woods. The peasants wore nets of tarred horsehair over their heads to protect themselves. So did I, for that matter.

"But I didn't care. I was busy studying—*Capital,* by Marx, of course, and old, dog-eared copies of *Iskra,* the organ of the Russian Social Democratic Labor Party, which were smuggled to us by comrades, all across Russia from Vienna. Also, I had an old issue of *Vperiod,* from 1905, which included an essay by Vladimir Ilich against Parvus called 'Should We

Organize the Revolution?' I did a little writing myself, besides; two pieces, which weren't very good, for a Populist Irkutsk newspaper, the *Vostochnoye Obozreniye.* I had to keep brushing those cockroaches from the sheets of paper. I drowned one in my inkwell. The important thing was to keep busy, to work. For some of the comrades, though, it didn't help."

"What happened to them?"

"They couldn't take the climate and the loneliness. And you could never tell, beforehand, which ones would crack. One of the best, for example, by the name of Yefimov, was a railroad worker, tough as nails. He spent all of his time studying, too." He smiled. " 'I'm a ratiolist,' he'd say, meaning 'rationalist.' 'That's what Marx has done for me.'

"At the end of the summer, just before I was sent to Verkholensk, he hanged himself from a pine tree in the forest, with a rope greased with lard."

"How did you finally escape?" Feibush asked.

"That was from Verkholensk, the following spring, just before the thaw. But it's a long story and it's getting late. We have to go. I'll tell you about it some other time."

"Have a glass of tea first," Mrs. Tauber said. "But I haven't got an apple, I'm afraid."

"Another time, thanks." He and Hannele got up to leave.

I said to him, "Roman Osipovich, could I speak with you alone for a minute? It's very important."

"Can't it wait?"

"No, it can't."

"All right," he said. "If you insist."

We sat on my folding cot. The sputtering candle between us lit up his face; he already had some wrinkles under his eyes.

"What's the trouble?" he asked.

"Keep your voice down," I told him. "The door won't shut. They can hear us in the kitchen."

He whispered, "Then tell me what this is all about."

"You can't go back home."

"Where? To Russia?"

"No," I said. "To Broome Street tonight."

"Why not?"

"Because Schlifka knows you're there."

A blob of melted wax quivered in the dish. He touched it with his finger and asked, "And how does he know that?"

"Because I told him."

"You?"

"Yes," I said.

"When?"

"Tonight."

"But why?"

"For money. He paid me twenty bucks for the information."

"How did you find out where we live?"

"I followed you."

"I see."

"No, you don't," I said. "Twenty bucks is a month's wages for me, working twelve, fourteen hours a day."

"What do you do?"

"I'm a presser."

"At your age?"

"I'm lucky to have the job."

"Yes, I guess you are, at that," he said. "Hannele tells me that you're all alone."

"I do okay."

"Then answer me this," he said. "Why're you tipping me off? You could have kept the money and your mouth shut. Nobody would have known the difference."

"Don't worry," I said. "I kept the twenty bucks. I can use it."

"You could still have kept your mouth shut. Why're you telling me this?"

"I've got my reasons," I said.

"That's fair enough."

"Are you sore at me?"

"No," he said. "Why should I be? It wasn't your fault."

"Then whose fault was it?"

"That's another long story," he said. "Sometime I'll explain it to you."

"Why not now?"

"No, there isn't time. But I promise you that I'll do it one of these days, very soon. There's one thing you can do for yourself, though, to help."

"What's that?"

"Read my articles in *Die Wahrheit,*" he said. "Start with the one tomorrow."

"I'll do that."

He stood up. The candle sputtered. "We've got to go now," he said.

"Have you got a place to stay?"

"Don't worry about us," he said. "Worry about

yourself. Schlifka's no fool. You're going to be in a lot of trouble when he finds out what you did."

"Don't I know it."

"In a day or two, maybe less, when he puts two and two together, he's going to come after you."

"I can take care of myself."

"You'll need help," he said. "Do you know the Café Neva on East Broadway?"

"The one right across the street from the Educational Alliance?"

"That's the place. There's a waiter there, a comrade of mine, by the name of Sasha. You can't miss him; he's very thin, with pop eyes. Jumpy, but I trust him. If you're in trouble, get in touch with him immediately. Tell him that Ivan Vasilyevich sent you; he'll tell you where to find me. Make sure that you're not followed, though."

"I'll be very careful."

"Come and stay with us as long as you like," he said. "You'll be safe with us."

"Thanks."

"For what?" he asked. "I owe you Hannele's life."

"Can I ask you a question?"

"That depends."

"Why don't you just kill Schlifka and have done with it?"

"It's not so easy to kill somebody," he said. "And it's too risky. If I'm caught, I'll probably be deported to Russia. You know what that would mean?"

"No."

"A cell in the Peter and Paul fortress, chains, the *nagaika* . . . Do you know what a *nagaika* is?"

"Yes. A Cossack whip."

He went on. "And a lot of questions from the specialists in the Okhrana about my political activities. They've been itching to get their hands on me for years."

"What's the Okhrana?" I asked.

"The secret police."

"The ones who wear those pea-green overcoats?"

"That's right," he said. "How did you know that?"

"They checked our papers at Myslowice, at the border, on the Russian side. I knew they weren't ordinary soldiers."

He opened the door; I blew the candle out.

In the kitchen Feibush was saying, "He was always a mama's boy; never very strong. He'll never make it."

I said to Roman Osipovich, "How come you use the name Ivan Vasilyevich? Is he someone you know?"

"I used to, very well, when I was a kid. He was a peasant who worked on my father's farm in Bobrinets."

"Your father was a farmer?"

"Yes," he said. "And a damn good one, too. Ivan Vasilyevich was a very old man, over eighty, when I knew him. He'd served twenty-five years as a private in the army under Nicholas I. He taught me a lot about life in Russia. My father, too," he added. "I mustn't forget about him. You could say, I suppose, that my father taught me the rest."

The next morning, on the trolley going to work, I read his latest article in *Die Wahrheit* but couldn't make head or tail of it. He called for the union, into one Russian Social Democratic Party, of "the hards and the softs," as he put it. Who the hell were they? He was also against the "expropriations" by the Bolsheviks, particularly in the Caucasus. What did that mean?

What stuck with me for good, though, was the last paragraph, in which he wrote about "the iron laws of History, revealed by the Dialectic which governs the Universe itself, that will eventually liberate the human race from Capitalist exploitation: the slavery of those condemned to make bricks without straw."

I happen to remember that, word for word, because as I got off the trolley at the corner of Pitt Street, I almost stepped on a horse's turd; there were wisps of straw in it.

What was the Dialectic? I couldn't get it out of my mind. It was already very warm. Did the sun, too, obey those universal laws? And what about the moon and the stars? I thought about it all day long.

At the same time, heading home that evening, I kept my eyes open for Schlifka or anyone else who might have been following me. There was no one.

Mrs. Tauber and Feibush were in the kitchen with Tofetsky. His kid was sitting on the floor under the table, banging a spoon against an iron frying pan.

"Stop it, Motele," Tofetsky yelled, but the kid kept it up. Then his father said, "She's gone without a trace." He blew his nose between his fingers, smeared with ink.

"Missing," he said. "For three weeks now, almost a month. It'll be a month next Tuesday. This morning

I got back in the mail the last money order I sent through Jarmulowsky's; the third in a row, in those yellow envelopes stamped, *'Adresse unbekannt.'* "

"Maybe she moved," Feibush said.

"She would have gone back to the place on Bernhard Strasse to pick up the money," he said. "She had to. It was all she had to live on."

"Then maybe she's sick and in a hospital."

"I had HIAS, the office in Hamburg, check that out," Tofetsky said. "There's no record of her there, in any hospital, anywhere. Even in Altona."

The kid banged his spoon against the pan. Tofetsky said, "That's the funny part of the whole business. That's why she couldn't come with us. Not because I didn't have the money, but because she was sick. Not seriously, you understand, just eye trouble. A kind of tic, if you know what I mean; a twitch she had in both eyes for a little more than a year. The day before we sailed, when we were all vaccinated, the German doctor who examined her said that meant she had worms. In her stomach, of all places.

" 'What's that got to do with her eyes?' I asked him, but all he said was, 'No good. She can't go.' He wrote something down on her inspection card, which he showed to some official who was there from the U.S. Consulate, who agreed. 'She can't go,' he said in German.

"What could I do? Take the family back to Lemberg? Things are very bad there. It took me almost four years to scrape up enough money for our passage. I thought, I'll go to the States alone, but that wasn't any good. It meant leaving Udel in Hamburg with the two kids, in that boardinghouse crawling with lice and bedbugs. Motele was covered with bites; some of them were already infected. Then I figured, I'll send Udel and Motele here and stay with Rochele. But that was no good either. How would a woman and a three-year-old kid manage alone in New York? What would she do? She'd never be able to make enough, taking care of the kid, to stay alive, much less give him a chance, a decent start in life. I had twenty-four hours—less—to make up my mind. Udel was frantic, no help at all. But Rochele said, 'You take them, Papa; go. I'll be all right here. It won't be forever.'

"Then the agent for the line took me aside in the waiting room and gave me an idea. 'Cash in her ticket,' he said. And he promised, for 10 percent, to take her to a doctor he knew, a famous specialist, on the Binnen-Alster, near some fancy hotel—the Atlantic, I think it was—who would cure her. 'What's worms?' he said. 'I have a dog who once had worms. It's nothing. She'll be fine in no time.'

"He also promised to arrange for her to stay at our boardinghouse at a reduced rate: two kronen a day for meals and board, and in a private room at that, in the attic. 'Believe me,' he said. 'It's your best bet.' I believed him."

"Did you get his name?" Feibush asked.

"Of course I got it. Herr Bubenden. He gave me his card, too, with his address on it. And he promised to write me, care of the Hamburg-American Line, after the doctor examined her. As soon as we got to New York, I went to the Line's office on Broadway every day. Nothing.

"After six weeks, I had them cable him—I had to

pay for that, too—at his office and his home. When the answers came—also out of my own pocket—the office over there said that he hadn't worked for them in over a month. He'd quit. His landlady—he lived in a pension on Holzdamm Strasse—said he moved away about the same time and didn't leave a forwarding address.

"I wasn't too worried because my money orders were still being cashed by Rochele. Then, three weeks ago, I got the first one back. And then another. I cabled the Hamburg police, direct, and asked them to look into it. So far, I haven't gotten an answer from them. That was a week and a half ago."

He blew his nose again into his ink-stained fingers, wiped them on his pants, and handed Feibush a buck.

"Keep it," Tofetsky said. "It might come in handy."

"What for?"

The kid banged away. "What're you going to do?" Feibush asked.

"I don't know," he said. "I'm not sure."

"Cable the police there again."

"I did, today."

"She'll turn up."

"No, I don't think so," he said. "Not any more."

The kid dropped the frying pan on the floor; startled by the clang, he burst out crying. Tofetsky picked him up. "What am I doing here?" he asked. "That's what I want to know. How did I wind up in America? Before I got married, it was Eretz Yisroel for me. I mean it. I was the only Zionist in Lemberg. That's because I read *The Jewish State* by Dr. Herzl when I was nineteen. A pamphlet, just eighty pages long—but nicely printed; what you call in America Gothic type. A well-designed frontispiece, too. It was published by somebody called Breitenstein in Vienna, a bookseller. Not Jewish, either. That's where I found it: in Vienna, at a book stall near the Ring. In my business, you know, you read a lot. It becomes a habit, like smoking. I read Dr. Herzl and was convinced, just like that—overnight. We Jews need a homeland of our own. We must redeem ourselves. I even brushed up on my Hebrew and subscribed to *HaZernan,* a Zionist paper published in Petersburg. But I got married and had kids instead."

The kid was asleep in his arms. I went to my room.

Just as I closed my eyes there was a knock on my door. It was Mrs. Tauber, holding a lighted candle. She was wearing her kimono, which she held closed above her breasts with her left hand.

"Can I speak with you a minute?" she asked.

"Sure."

She remained in the open doorway. "I've decided to rent the parlor to Feibush," she said. "There are rats in the basement. Reb Rosen got bitten on the nose."

"I hadn't heard."

"It happened last night. The tip was bitten off. He almost bled to death. Feibush stopped the bleeding, before the doctor came, with a cobweb."

"A cobweb?"

"Yes, it's apparently an old carpenter's trick."

I heard a thump at the end of the hall, to her right, and something heavy being dragged across the floor.

"Can I help?"

"No, I don't think so."

"The parlor's a nice room," I said. I pictured the oilcloth on the floor, the round-topped table, the Morris chair covered with peeling imitation leather, and, above all, the folding davenport against the wall, under the gas jet.

"It's got a nice view, too," I said.

"Yes, it gets a little sunlight late in the afternoon."

"Well, I hope he'll be happy here."

"I'm sure he will," she said.

"You too."

She smiled. "Yes, me too," she said.

I fell asleep, then woke again at the creak of a floorboard in the hall. I went to the door and peeked out. It was too dark to see anything. A board creaked again, farther away, and at the end of the long hallway the parlor door opened halfway. Feibush was standing there in his undershirt. The gas jet, turned very low, lit up only one side of his face. And then the door opened wider and I saw Mrs. Tauber in front of him, wearing her kimono. It was pale blue. She stretched out her arms. The wide sleeves blocked my view. All I could see was the top of Feibush's head, one of his bare feet, and the glossy cushion on the back of the Morris chair behind him, to his left.

7

THREE DAYS LATER, on Thursday afternoon, Tofetsky came home from work at four and took gas, as we say in Yiddish. He killed himself in the kitchen by stuffing two wet shirts in the crack under the door and turning on the jet over the sink.

I got home, as usual, at seven. Feibush, who was holding Motele on his lap, gave him a lump of yellow sugar, put him down on the kitchen floor, and took me in the hallway to the parlor.

"His wife and kid got back from shopping at a little after six. He was sitting in a chair with his head on the table and one arm hanging down," he said. "She tried to bring him around, but it wasn't any use. He'd planned the whole thing very carefully."

"But why?"

"He got a cable this morning from the Hamburg police. They couldn't find any trace of his daughter. The paper was on the table when Udel found him. Miriam was here, too."

"Where are they now?"

"At the morgue, identifying the body."

The kid finally passed out on the davenport, with his thumb in his mouth. His mother picked him up at midnight; her eyes were red. She kept grimacing and sucking in her breath through her clenched teeth.

When she left, Mrs. Tauber filled us in on the rest of the story: the cop on the beat nosing around, the clanging in the street. The two women followed the black death wagon to the morgue on Twenty-sixth Street in a hackney; it cost Mrs. Tauber a buck and a quarter. The corpse, covered with a tarpaulin, was laid out on three blocks of ice.

"It took hours to fill in all the papers," she said. "Then we had to identify him. I made them take Udel outside and then some man in a dirty white coat, wearing rubber gloves, showed me the face. It was bright red—brick-colored—the lips, too, and all smeared with Vaseline. I don't know why. Also, the mouth was wide open." She added, "The ice was melting; there was a big puddle of water on the floor."

"What about the funeral?" Feibush asked.

"That's a problem. He didn't belong to a burial society, and she doesn't have a dime to her name. The man in the white coat telephoned a Jewish undertaker by the name of Radek, on Eldridge Street, who told me that he'd take care of the whole thing for fourteen dollars. I told him twelve was as high as we could go, and he finally agreed. It'll be tomorrow afternoon at three, and he'll be buried in the Union Fields Cemetery in Jamaica."

"That's where my father is," I said.

She went on, "We can pay it out in weekly installments of two dollars, or all at once. I told him all at once. How much can you spare?" she asked Feibush.

"Two bucks," he said. "No, three."

"I've got four. We'll have to get the rest from the people in the building."

"I'll get on it right away," he said, standing up.

"I'd like to help some," I said.

"You can."

"How much?"

"Not with money," she said. "You and old man Isaacs get along pretty well, don't you?"

"Okay, I guess."

"I want you to go and ask him to prepare the body," she said. "Udel wants it done properly. It's important to her."

"Why don't you get Ostrovsky to ask him?"

"He wouldn't."

"How come?"

"Because he says the old man won't do it. It's forbidden, because Tofetsky was a suicide."

"Then why would he listen to me?"

"He probably won't," she said. "But we have to try."

"Have you got a pack of Tolstoys?" I asked.

"On the kitchen table."

"I'll try my best," I said.

The old man listened, smoking three cigarettes in a row, and then said no.

There was a book open on the kitchen table. "No," he repeated. "I can't. The Law is clear. The *Shulhan Aruk* says clearly that one who willfully kills himself is not attended to. One does not mourn for him, tear one's clothes. We recite the mourner's blessing, yes; we give comfort to the mourners, of course, but whatever is done for the sake of the dead, we don't do. Only a child who commits suicide is exempt; it's considered as if he has done it unintentionally."

"Then what about someone like King Saul?" I asked.

He took the cigarette out of his mouth, narrowed his wrinkled lids, and stared at me. "Yes," he said. "That's true. Saul, too, was an exception."

"How come?"

"Because it's considered that he was under intolerable pressure. Under those circumstances, suicide is regarded as unintentional and we hold nothing back from the dead." He raised his right hand. "But that has nothing to do with Reb Tofetsky, may God forgive him. Yes, I know the whole story about his daughter. It's terrible. But no excuse."

"Why not?"

"For one thing, he had his wife and child to consider," he said, closing the book. "For another, you're asking me to break our holy Law."

"Yes."

"But the Law is all we have."

"Is it?"

"Yes, particularly now when, as it is written, the Day of the Lord is at hand."

"Where does it say that?"

"Reach over there, behind you on the shelf, and hand me the book with the cloth cover."

"This one?"

"The one next to it," he said, dropping his cigarette on the floor and grinding it out with his heel. He wet his forefinger on the tip of his tongue, flipped through the yellowing pages, stopped, and read aloud in Hebrew, " 'Israel speaks to God: When will you redeem us? He answers: When you have sunk to the lowest level, at that time will I redeem you.' Do you understand what that means?"

"No."

"It means—and, God help you, you'll live to see this—that the mirror you hold up in your hand will reflect someone else's face. That Esau, covered with the hair of a goat, will unsheathe his sword, and Israel . . . Yes, it's true. The War of Gog and Magog is coming, and the soldiers of Edom . . . One of them will ride in a black car, and in a huge ditch, in the field on his left . . . No, a mound of earth, a fresh grave, filled with Jews, some living, some dead . . . The earth will move . . . The footprints, all the footprints of the soldiers' boots, in the soft earth, will fill up with Jewish blood . . ."

I gave him another cigarette. He lit it, took a drag, and asked, "Have you seen Hannele recently?"

"Not recently, no."

"If you run into her, would you do me a favor?"

"If I can."

"Give her this," he said. "She forgot it," and he took from his pant pocket her tortoise-shell comb, from which a tooth was missing.

I told Mrs. Tauber it was no go.

She said, "It's what I expected."

We waited up in the parlor for Feibush, who came back a little after two.

"I got it," he said. "More. Twenty-four bucks, all told."

I never made the funeral. Getting off the trolley on Pitt Street the following morning, I spotted Schlifka on the cast-iron steps of the building where I worked. I hid behind three barrels of herring pickled in brine, and then made a dash between two cars across the street, and got on a trolley headed back west.

Luck was with me. He hadn't seen me. Through the window streaked with dirt, I saw him giving a girl the once-over. She had on a hat with two black ostrich feathers.

I made straight for home as fast as I could, where I stuffed my sheepskin jacket along with my other things into my valise and tied it up with a piece of rope—part of a clothesline I found in the kitchen. I thought about leaving Mrs. Tauber a note and looked in the parlor for a pencil and paper; nothing. It was just as well. I couldn't tell her where I was going and I was ashamed to say why.

Halfway out the front door, I went back again, and into her bedroom, where I opened her underwear drawer, took out her velvet sachet stuffed with dried rose petals, and stuck it in my pocket. I left the house key on the kitchen table.

Mrs. Tofetsky's door was open; I saw an old lady, who lived on the second floor, with a bowl of eggs in her hands. Mr. Rosen was there, too, with a bandaged nose. He said, "I'll go and get some," as I ran down the stairs.

There was one customer at the Neva Café on East Broadway. He was reading the Yiddish weekly *Die Neue Freie Presse* over a glass of tea. Sasha was easy to recognize in his white apron. He was slicing up a lemon on a table in the back. I walked over and waited for him to finish.

"Something I can do for you?" he asked.

"Ivan Vasilyevich sent me."

"So you're the one," he said, laying out the slices on a plate. "Well, any comrade of Ivan Vasilyevich is a comrade of mine."

"Can you tell me where I can find him?"

"That all depends."

"On what?"

His pop eyes flitted from my face to the front door. "Are you sure you weren't followed here?" he asked.

"Positive."

"Check again."

I went to the window, stood to one side, and looked out.

"What about that beggar on crutches?" he asked.

"I never saw him before in my life," I said. "Will you help me?"

"We'll see what can be arranged."

8

I HID OUT with Hannele and Roman Osipovich for two weeks in their three-room apartment on the top floor of a building on Broadway, between Broome and Grand Streets. Hannele answered the door when I arrived. She was wearing a blouse with a high collar and a long pleated skirt. We had boiled noodles for lunch.

At around seven or so, the three of us were in the parlor; the window faced west. Hannele and I were on the brocade divan. Roman Osipovich was sitting behind a table; it was covered with papers on which sentences in Yiddish were scrawled in ink and scratched out. While we talked, I noticed that his eyes, magnified by the pince-nez, were fixed on a patch of sunlight between us on the wooden floor. It began to fade. He lifted the white glass mantle and lit the gas jet. But when the sunlight was gone, he jumped up again and walked out of the room, slamming the door behind him.

"Would you believe it?" Hannele said. "He's scared of the dark."

"Roman Osipovich?"

"Ever since he was a kid. Not so much the dark, but the twilight, when the sun goes down."

An hour later, in the middle of supper, the front door opened and a guy came in and sat down at the kitchen table without a word. He was tall and thin, with a two- or three-day growth of beard; it was darker than his hair. Hannele put a plate of steaming noodles in front of him.

"This is Stenka Petrovich," Roman Osipovich said to me. "Another comrade who's staying with us. He doesn't understand any Yiddish."

I shook his calloused hand. With his mouth stuffed with noodles, he said something in Russian to Roman Osipovich. Later on, he puffed on his pipe. It was a curved Meerschaum, with a fancy nickel band around the celluloid stem—obviously brand-new. He smoked tobacco from American cigarettes: three Sweet Caporals, which he shredded into the bowl between his blunt fingers.

"He just bought it at Wanamaker's," Roman Osipovich told me. "He's breaking it in."

The pipe finally went out. He knocked the bowl against his palm, emptying the ashes on his plate, on which he'd dropped the burned matches and cigarette papers rolled into tiny balls. Over tea, he filled it up again, with three more shredded cigarettes, and tamped down the tobacco with the long, dirty nail on his forefinger. And after that, with the pipe between his teeth, he left the apartment for a while.

He was always going out for a while, at all hours of the day and night. No matter when he came back, he and Roman Osipovich went into the parlor and shut the door.

They were in there late one afternoon when Hannele said to me, "He gives me the creeps."

"Who is he?" I asked. "What's he doing here?"

I was sitting on my folding cot in the alcove.

"God knows," she said. "Making contacts, I think. Collecting stuff. Letters and things to smuggle back into Russia. He was one of the ones who held up the *Nicholas I.*"

"What's that?"

"A big ship, carrying a lot of money, in the port of Baku," she said. "He did it for the Party."

"Which party?"

"The Bolsheviks."

"I thought Roman Osipovich was against the Bolsheviks."

"He is and he isn't," she said. "He can't make up his mind. He broke with the Mensheviks, too, in 1905."

"Who're they?"

"The 'softs,' " she said. "That's what the Bolsheviks call them."

I said, "So Stenka Petrovich is a 'hard.' "

"He spent five years in chains, working in a gold mine somewhere in Siberia; I forget what the place is called."

"What's he want from Roman Osipovich?"

"He wants him to join his party."

"Will he?"

"I don't know," she said. "He tells me . . . I can't make head or tail of it. He doesn't object to the Bolsheviks on moral grounds. It's . . . You've heard him carry on. He believes . . . I'm not quite sure, but he and the Bolsheviks have different ideas about certain things. I don't know what. He sometimes reminds me of Papa, studying Cabala. They're both convinced they know some secret, and that makes them . . ." She laughed. "Papa and his Cabala. Only it's not funny," she said. "I sometimes hate Papa for believing in God, for loving Him so. At the same time, I understand it." She twisted a strand of her dark hair around her finger. "Only too well."

"Which reminds me," I said. "Your papa asked me to return your comb."

"Thank you."

"You're welcome."

"Did he say anything about me?"

"He sent you his love."

"Did he really?" she asked. "No, I don't believe it. But you're nice for saying so. It's very sweet. Does he know where I am?"

"No."

"He doesn't care much for Roman Osipovich, you know," she said. "Do you think Papa knows what happened between me and Schlifka?"

"Not a chance of it," I said.

"Honestly?"

"No idea at all."

"Well, thank God for small favors," she said. "And thank you again. I've had this ever since I was a little girl. It's real tortoise shell, not an imitation."

"One of the teeth is broken."

"I know," she said. "But I can't bring myself to throw it away."

With her head to one side, she ran the comb through her hair. Her lips remained parted; her brown eyes were narrowed, exactly like her old man's. Then she said, "It's late. I've got to fix supper."

"What're we having?"

"Guess."

"Noodles again."

"Wrong," she said. "Kasha, but boiled in water. We're out of milk."

"Do you want me to go down and get some?"

"No. Save your money. Water's good enough."

I said, "Before I forget, here's my share for the week," and handed her a buck.

We lived communally, sharing everything, each contributing as much as he could afford. Roman Osipovich wrote five or six articles a week for *Die Wahrheit,* for which he got a dollar apiece. He also did a weekly column, under the name Lyubka, for *Die Neue Freie Presse,* which brought in another dollar.

I've no idea how much Stenka Petrovich kicked in. He had one shirt to his name—a Russian blouse with a high collar, from which both buttons were missing. I never saw him buy anything for himself but cigarettes—except a bottle of Eastman's Violet Toilet Water he doused on his sandy hair every morning. For some reason, he was crazy about the smell of violets. It was better than his sweat, which stank to high heaven. Early in the week, I overheard Hannele complain to Roman Osipovich about that.

He said, "You must understand, his father was born a serf."

"What's that got to do with it? I can't stand him near me. Take him to the steam bath on Allen Street for a sweat."

"I can't do that."

"Why not?"

"We're comrades. The suggestion would be an insult."

"Well, then at least take the kid. He stinks, too."

He laughed. "Tomorrow after I finish work; I promise."

It set us back a quarter apiece. First, in the two front rooms we soaked for ten or fifteen minutes in iron bathtubs filled with hot water. Next, in the back we sat naked side by side on one of the wooden benches facing the brick kiln, heated by coal, which was filled with large, smooth stones. Every once in a while the Russian attendant splashed a bucket of cold water on them, which hissed and sent up clouds of steam. Roman Osipovich's glasses clouded up.

"I can't see anything," he said.

"Me neither."

For another nickel each, the attendant lashed us with his *besomel*—a bunch of leafy eucalyptus twigs. He chatted in Russian with Roman Osipovich.

"What do you know about that?" he told me. "He's from Petersburg, too. An island in the Neva. He could see the Peter and Paul from his roof."

"Is that so?"

"He was a worker," Roman Osipovich said. "A lathe operator. One of those who went out on strike in 1905."

"What's he doing here?"

"He lost hope," he said.

"How does he like New York?"

"Okay, I guess. He's married and has two kids in school. A boy and a girl. They can't speak Russian any more."

"That's no loss."

"No, you're wrong," he said. "It's a great language."

"So's English."

"Yes, but not for the children of a Russian worker."

The twigs lashed my back; another bucket of water splashed and hissed on the hot stones.

"Is that what you consider yourself?" I asked Roman Osipovich. "A Russian?"

"A Russian Social Democrat."

"Not a Jew?"

"How can I be a Jew? I'm a materialist. In the Party we're all the same: Great Russians, Ukrainians, Georgians, Jews. There's no difference between us. Russia is our country, for the time being. But one day, after the Revolution, we'll be citizens of the world. The Party, you see, is the vanguard of the future: the classless society, where nationalities . . . They won't matter any more. Anti-Semitism, for example, won't exist."

"I'd like to believe it."

"Do," he said.

Hannele never left the apartment. She cooked, cleaned, after a fashion, did our laundry, and stared out the parlor window.

"Look at that," she called to me one morning, and we watched a bright red Pierce Arrow, with front doors, shift gears and head up Broadway. It was driven by a chauffeur wearing goggles, white gauntlets, and a cap with a shiny black visor. There was no one in the back seat.

"Wouldn't you love to own one of those?" she asked me.

"I sure would."

"It'd be fun to be rich, no matter what Roman Osipovich says."

He and I took turns shopping on Broadway late every afternoon. "Keep your eyes open," he said, and I did. There was no sign of Schlifka. Once, though, from a distance I noticed a fat blonde hanging around outside the grocery on Grand Street. It turned out she was a nutty Polack who mumbled to herself.

A couple of times a week we had to leave Hannele alone; I was out shopping and Roman Osipovich had some research to do at the Cooper Union Reading Room. Hannele locked the apartment from the inside with the latch and chain. We had to knock twice, wait, and knock again before she'd open up.

One evening, around seven, Roman Osipovich came home with a round, ten-pound loaf of black bread he'd bought in the bakery up the street. Hannele took one look at him and asked, "Are you okay?"

"I'm tired," he said, handing her the bread. "I think I'll stretch out for a few minutes."

"The vodka is under the bed."

He lit the kerosene lamp on the kitchen table and carried it across the hall to their bedroom, where there was no gas. I heard his footsteps and watched the light move back and forth in the crack under the door. The bedsprings creaked. Stenka Petrovich wandered into the kitchen for a glass of tea. Hannele cut him a slice of bread. A half hour later Roman Osipovich joined us, carrying the lamp; his face and neck were flushed from the booze. Stenka Petrovich puffed on his pipe.

That night at supper we had a guest whose name I didn't catch. He was very pale and his head was shaved, which made his ears stick out. He had a peculiar habit of speaking very quietly, hardly moving his lips. He and Roman Osipovich hugged and then kissed each other on the cheeks.

"This is my second night out," he whispered. "The traffic—all those motorcars—makes me jump. I'm scared to cross the street. I can't get used to it."

"You will," Roman Osipovich told him. "Just give yourself a little time."

"I hope you're right."

In the kitchen, he asked, "And who's this?"

"This is Comrade Hannele," Roman Osipovich said.

"She's very pretty. Mazeltov."

We had kasha boiled in water again. The pale guy wolfed it down.

"There isn't any more," Hannele told him. "I'm sorry. How about some more bread?"

"Fine."

"Take two slices."

"Yes, I will, thank you," he said, biting off a chunk.

"Was it bad?" Roman Osipovich asked him.

He chewed, swallowed, and said, "No. The worst thing was being out of touch with your comrades. That got to me after a while. But after all, it was only for a year. What's a year out of a man's life?" He bit on another thick slice of bread. "Longer, I think, would have been a problem for me. The lack of intellectual stimulation."

Roman Osipovich translated this for Stenka Petrovich; he took his pipe out of his mouth and laughed.

The pale guy said, "Yes, I know. It sounds . . ." He ran his hand over his shaved scalp. "But it was all something quite new to me, you see," he said. "I wasn't . . ."

I had to lean forward to catch his words; so did Hannele, who was sitting on my left. It turned out that he'd just been sprung from Blackwell's Island—for what, he never said. But it was all mixed up in that shaved head: handcuffs, rusty clippers, the cell in the police station on Mulberry Street which stank from piss; the one on the Island with an iron cot.

"The blankets were burlap," he said. "They made us wear white, striped uniforms. Once a day, in the late afternoon, we were marched by the guards to the river to empty our slop buckets. Oh my God, what a stink. But the path to the water—it was gravel—was lined by trees, like a beautiful park."

Stenka Petrovich, for whom all this was being translated, burst out laughing again. But the pale guy kept going.

"And the food," he said. "For breakfast, a slice of bread, a stale crust, and a tin of warm brown water to drink. The cop beat me on the kidneys with his billy; the one on Mulberry Street, I mean. In the cell next door—this is on the Island—there was an anarchist who knew Berkman. We argued all the time."

Then he added, "The whores on dope, screaming in their cells all night long. That was the worst. We slipped them cigarettes whenever we could."

"That was very kind of you," Hannele said.

"No, not at all."

"But it was."

"No, to be honest, we did it to shut them up."

"I can understand that, can't you?" she asked Roman Osipovich.

The pale guy said, "The lunatics were worse."

Stenka Petrovich said something in Russian, which made Roman Osipovich say to Hannele and me, "We've got things to talk about. Would you excuse us?"

I went into the parlor alone for a few minutes and looked out the window at the lights. On my way to my cot in the alcove, I passed Hannele's open door.

"Come on in a minute," she said. "Would you like a drink? There's a little vodka left."

"Thanks very much."

She was leaning back against the brass bedstead, running her comb through her hair. Her feet were bare. She handed me the bottle and said, "There's not much left, I'm afraid. Roman Osipovich had it bad tonight."

"So I noticed," I said. "What's he so scared of?"

"I don't know," she said. "He won't tell me."

I took a swallow from the bottle—it was the real Russian stuff—and she said, "Go ahead. Finish it off."

"Thanks."

"Stenka Petrovich is going back to Russia next Monday, did you know that?"

"No."

"He'll take Feibush's letter with him."

"Good luck to him," I said.

"He'll need it," she said. "And so will Roman Osipovich. He's going back soon, too. He told me last night. In about two months. He's stopping off in Zurich to see some people on the way."

"Are you going with him?"

"I've thought about it," she said.

"If they catch him, he's in for trouble."

"I know that," she said. "But that wouldn't stop me."

She put the empty bottle on the floor. "Nothing would stop me—if there was anything between us. He never touches me, you know; we sleep side by side, night after night in this bed, but he never lays a hand on me. I don't know why. I guess he thinks that after Schlifka . . . He's right. I'm glad. No, he's right and wrong at the same time. Does that make any sense to you? I guess not. It was very strange . . . what happened with Schlifka. Am I embarrassing you?"

"No, of course not."

"You're a good kid," she said.

"Tell me about Schlifka."

"Sure. Why not?"

She drew up her knees, clasped her hands around them, and told me how Schlifka had brought back something she'd forgotten for years: a daydream she'd had at twelve, right after her mother's death, when her father became rabbi of that shul near the Lubyankovka cemetery.

She said, "He spent all his time, day and night, translating from the Zohar and praying. And when he prayed, I swear, you could see the vein throb in his neck. Sometimes, when he saw me, he wept, kissed the palms of my hands, and held them up to his heart. But I developed very early, and after that, because I had irregular periods, he never touched me; not once, if he could help it.

"One time, I remember, in the spring, when he knew I was having my period, I was watering some lilacs that grew in our little garden just behind the house. His window was open and he saw me. He leaned out and yelled, 'Don't. Do you want to poison them? You'll kill them.'

"I dropped the pitcher; it broke on a stone. I believed everything he told me, and I loved God. Have you ever loved God?"

"Yes."

"Then you know what it's like," she said. "The joy. And the fear. All I wanted was to serve Him, obey His holy commandments. And, if possible, die for the Sanctification of His Name."

"Me too."

"There was always a chance of it. We barely escaped from the pogrom in Kiev in 1905. But we did, and so I served Him the only way I could. I learned the women's prayers, how to stick my finger up a chicken's kishkas to see if it was kosher, I went to mikvah, and, in my spare time, studied those little Yiddish chapbooks written for girls that Papa occasionally bought from a peddler for a few kopeks. There's nothing left in that bottle, is there?"

"No."

"I could use a drink," she said. "Anyway, I read one of those chapbooks in particular, again and again. It was about a pious Jewish girl of about sixteen or so whose family had been killed by Chmielnicki's Cossacks in Lublin during the massacres—when were they? Years and years ago. But she was a virgin and so beautiful that Bogdan Chmielnicki had her brought to his tent. The guards threw her inside on some cushions. 'The hetman is coming,' they said. 'Tonight, the hetman will be here.' They left her alone for an hour or so. She bit off the tip of her tongue and choked herself to death on the blood."

"Is such a thing possible?"

"I don't know, but I believed it," she said. "I learned the story by heart, word for word—the girl's name, I remember, was Sarah. But then, despite myself, I began to change it here and there, little by little. Soon I imagined that I was Chmielnicki's slave. He wore a gold ring in one ear. Oh yes, he had a shaved head, too, and on his feet, up to his knees, soft boots made from red Moroccan leather—the finest—with little gold tassels hanging from the top, in front. I imagined . . . I don't know what . . . I was very ignorant . . . but he stripped me naked and made me kiss his curved saber. The steel blade was ice-cold. And then get down, on all fours, and lick those boots. Sometimes, though, when he came into the tent, he picked me up tenderly in his arms, rocked me back and forth against his chest, and kissed me on the eyelids . . . my mole . . . Once he brought me a comb made out of solid silver, on a velvet cushion, and a bracelet to match. Then, when I'd stuck the comb in my hair and slipped the bracelet on my right wrist, he kicked me in the stomach . . ."

She closed her eyes. "Schlifka brought it all back to me. Only he was real, in the flesh, stinking from sweat, bourbon, semen, his cigars, and that awful brilliantine. That was the realest thing of all: the way his hair smelled too sweet. He wasn't in my imagination, but there; his back is all covered with thick hair. He was a living God; not pure spirit, something I couldn't touch or taste or smell or feel.

"That's what I felt sometimes; not in so many words. Who knows? Maybe it was the drug in the booze. But sometimes, when he was done with me, I was grateful to him. Can you understand that?"

"Grateful for what?"

"For making me his slave, serving a God. He made me go down on my knees naked in front of him and suck on his shlang until it got hard, and then he jammed it down my throat and made me gag. Or I had to get down on all fours and stick up my ass. That didn't work, so he made me kneel on the bed with my head down and spread my cheeks. At first he used Vaseline; in a couple of days it wasn't necessary. It didn't hurt any more, not too badly, anyway. I didn't mind. I liked it. There were times, may God forgive me, when I loved him."

The next night, after supper, I was alone with Roman Osipovich in the parlor. He was rereading something he'd written on a yellow piece of paper.

"Did you ever kill anybody?" I asked.

He laughed. "No, not yet. Why?"

"Has Stenka Petrovich?"

"So they tell me."

"What did he do?"

"That I can't discuss," he said, going back to his reading.

"Why don't you ask Stenka Petrovich to kill Schlifka?"

"I've thought about it," he said.

"Then why don't you do it?"

"Because he'd refuse."

"How come?"

"It would be a breach of Party discipline," he said.

I have to explain that, during those two weeks, whenever he got the chance he spent time talking with me—generally after supper, in the parlor, for fifteen or twenty minutes. He tried to describe dialectical materialism. "We'll make it as simple as possible," he said, and told me about the universal laws of historical development: thesis, antithesis, and synthesis—something I grasped right away—along with things like the Theory of Surplus Value, which remains a mystery to me to this day.

What I also didn't understand was the "why." I kept asking, "How come the middle class will become pauperized?" and "Why will the state eventually wither away?"—questions like that, until one night I said, "It's wonderful, if it's true. But how do you know that History has a purpose?"

"From Marx."

"But how can you be sure that Marx is right?"

"From objective and subjective experience," he said. "Both."

"I don't understand what that means."

"From History and things that happened to me."

"What kind of things?"

"I've told you that my father was a farmer," he said. "He became a rich man. And how? By exploiting the peasants—particularly the migrant workers who came to us on foot from as far away as Kiev, to harvest the hay. The reapers. He hired about thirty of them every summer, if the harvest was good. They worked from dawn till midnight, by the light of torches, and he paid them forty rubles apiece. The men, that is; the women got half that. Oh yes, and free board, too, which meant the open fields in good weather, or under a haystack if it rained. And they had their children with them, you understand, babies, too. On those wages, they couldn't afford to eat meat—just millet soup and porridge.

" 'It's good enough for them,' Papa would tell me. 'What are they? They're animals.'

"His foreman was old Ivan Vasilyevich—I've told you about him, too."

"I remember."

"I loved that old man—his long white beard that covered his chest, his stories about the army. He fought in the Crimean War, if you can believe it, at Sevastopol. He loved me, too. Every spring, when the mud reached your knees, he carved me a pair of wooden galoshes—buskins, a kind of half-boot, which came up to my shins.

"But he was caught between my father and the workers. The summer I was twelve, some of them, maybe half, were stricken with night-blindness; as soon as it got dark, they couldn't see. It was because of their diet—and they knew it. I remember one in particular, a kid almost my own age, stumbling around our courtyard with his hands stretched out. Papa gave him a glass of vodka, and he passed out near the fence.

"But the workers had had enough. Not that they rebelled exactly—God forbid—but they all gathered one evening, just as it was getting dark, in our front yard. They wanted a little more money—just enough to be able to eat meat once a week, the Elder said. Papa called Ivan Vasilyevich and told him, 'Drive that drek out of here.' He spoke to him in a mixture of Russian, Ukrainian, and Yiddish; at home, with Mama and me, he spoke Yiddish. 'Do you hear me? Get rid of them,' he yelled.

"And old Ivan Vasilyevich shuffled out in the yard —he had stiff legs—and said, 'Brothers . . .'

"A young girl, about fifteen, standing up front, giggled; out of nervousness, really. But she couldn't stop. With her hands on her hips, she began laughing in the old man's face. I could see her clearly in the last rays of the sun coming through the leaves of the acacia trees. The men around her began laughing, too—some were drunk—and the girl, carried away, spit in the old man's face. He slapped her hard enough to knock her down.

"My father yelled from the porch, 'Good. That's the way,' and the rest of the peasants, without saying a word, went away. I could make out the blind boy —it was already that dark—with his hands on a man's shoulders. Ivan Vasilyevich wiped the spit from his beard with a kerchief; one, I remember, which had originally belonged to Mama.

"Three days later he was dead. The back of his head was blown off by a shotgun made from an old Berdan rifle . . ."

"Who did it?"

"A peasant. He was drunk. He tripped over a birch log, but he deliberately pulled the trigger. I saw it. Ivan Vasilyevich was five or six paces ahead of him; he hadn't turned around because he was hard of hearing. The peasant, on the ground, raised the gun to his shoulder, shut one eye, took aim, and fired. And Ivan Vasilyevich was out hunting with him, you know, for fresh meat: rabbits."

"Why didn't you turn him in?"

"I thought about it. It was on the tip of my tongue. The motive was clear. The police told us the peasant was the girl's uncle."

"Then why didn't you?"

"Because, while they were in the house, investigating the whole business, I realized it was Papa's fault. The whole thing. I never forgave him.

" 'Here, your honor,' he said to the officer who was wearing a saber. 'A little vodka to wet your whistle.' They drank half a bottle together, and ate a plate of pickled cucumbers. Mama brought them."

He didn't discover Marx, though, until he was nineteen, while studying to become an engineer in Odessa. One day, during a lecture, a fellow student, a Czech, slipped him a copy of *The Communist Manifesto.* He read it, then borrowed a copy of *Capital.*

"I couldn't put it down," he said. "The descriptions

of the conditions of the factory workers in industrial society brought back . . . It revived the greatest passion of my childhood: my indignation against my father and, by extension, the whole rotten capitalist system . . . the exploitation, which was responsible for the murder of Ivan Vasilyevich . . . everything. I made an astonishing discovery: my feelings and the purpose of History were in perfect accord. It was a revelation to me, blinding. What was I by myself? Nothing. An insect. Like that roach I drowned years later at Ust Kut. I stuck my pen point in it, under the wings. It took twenty minutes by my watch to drown. What's the difference between us? The human personality is just a subjective phenomenon which we must transcend. How? By surrendering the individual will to the historical dialectic. Which means the Party—I understand that now.

"By summer vacation I was a Marxist. I distributed copies of *Yuzhny Rabochy* to the workers in Odessa. When I went home in August for a week, I didn't fight with my father once. I wasn't angry with him any more. He couldn't help what he did. He acted according to his class interests. Well, so did everybody else, including me. I was a professional revolutionary. I almost felt sorry for him. His class is doomed; it'll be liquidated. The land belongs to the peasants. His house, too; the bed where he wants to die. He's getting on now. I hope he makes it."

At six Monday morning Stenka Petrovich walked out. In one hand, he had a cardboard suitcase tied up with string; the curved pipe was clenched between his teeth. Roman Osipovich left with him. He didn't get back till ten that night, when he said to me, "I saw Feibush and Miriam Tauber this evening. They send their regards."

"Thanks."

"They were very worried about you."

"Were they?"

"Not any more, though," he said. "I explained everything."

"Everything?"

"Yes," he said. "They'd like to see you."

"I doubt it."

"No, they would. They don't blame you for anything."

"I can't believe that," I said.

"Nobody blames you for anything."

"I don't want your forgiveness."

"It's not a question of forgiveness," he said. "Certainly not with me. You were exploited, like Hannele. Used for profit. That's nothing new in the world. You can't blame anyone for that."

"Is that what Mrs. Tauber said?"

"She said she wants to see you. I think you ought to go. It would be the nice thing to do. The polite thing. She and Feibush are getting married."

"I knew they would, sooner or later."

"Go wish them 'mazeltov,' " he said. "But be careful. Watch yourself."

I spent a long time outside the house on Orchard Street. The full moon shone on the dome of Jarmulowsky's bank at the end of the block. Finally, I went upstairs.

Feibush shook my hand; Mrs. Tauber kissed me on the forehead. "When's the lucky day?" I asked.

"Soon," she said. "No, don't go yet. Let's sit in the parlor."

"You've lost some weight," Feibush said. "But you've grown some, too, I swear."

"I'm fine."

"Are you very involved with Roman Osipovich?" Mrs. Tauber asked.

"Some."

"Don't get too involved," she said.

"Why not?"

"Nobody has all the answers," she said. "And besides, there are other things."

"Like what?"

"Ordinary things. Good food, clean clothes, a hot bath once in a while. And when the time comes, a decent girl. You'll fall in love, get married, and become a father."

"Maybe."

"Of course you will."

"That's how Mama died," I said.

"How?"

"Giving birth. It was another boy, who was born dead. Papa sent me outside when the midwife came, but I stood on my toes and looked through the window. You'd be surprised how much I can remember."

The following Wednesday evening Hannele and I were chatting in the kitchen when Roman Osipovich came back from delivering his weekly article to *Die Neue Freie Presse.* The iron pot, filled with noodles, bubbled on the stove. He lit the kerosene lamp, took it to their bedroom, and shut the door.

"Here, you'd better give him this," Hannele said, handing me a bottle of vodka from the shelf above the icebox. "But knock first."

"Come in," he said. He was on his back, with his hands behind his head; the lamp was beside the bed on the floor. "What is it?"

"From Hannele," I said.

He sat up, took a long pull, gave me back the bottle, and lay down again. I started to leave. A moth bumped against the chimney of the lamp. Staring at the huge shadow flitting on the wall, he said, "A drink or two helps, and lying down like this, with my hands behind my head. Sometimes—and I'm never sure when it'll happen—as the sun goes down and it begins to get dark, my palms sweat, my mouth goes dry, my heart pounds, and I'm filled . . . I'm scared of getting shot, you see. Having the back of my head blown off, like old Ivan Vasilyevich. Ridiculous, isn't it? But when it comes on, like tonight, I can feel the gun pointed at me . . . I don't know what kind; but not that old Berdan. Maybe a revolver; a Mauser or a Browning. I'm not sure. I've got no idea who's aiming it, either, but tonight, for example, as I crossed Essex Street right after the sun went down, I felt the muzzle on me. It was close, too; quite close. On the sidewalk I forced myself to turn around. There was no one there. Just a little kid at the curb, much younger than you. He was wearing a jacket in all that heat; one of his sleeves was patched with leather from the sole of a shoe. Then a woman went by. There was nobody else. It made no difference.

"All along East Broadway, in the shadows, it was the same thing. There was the muzzle of a loaded gun pointed at me from behind. Right here, at the base of the skull, exactly in the middle, between these two bones, like knobs, behind the ears . . .

"That's where Ivan Vasilyevich got his. Only that happened at noon, in the heat of the day. I've no idea why the darkness brings it on for me."

"How about another drink?"

"No, thanks," he said. "Just leave me alone for a while."

9

HANNELE SAID, "I'm sick and tired of noodles and kasha," so I made up my mind to buy a chicken, out of my own pocket, the next time I went shopping.

That was on Friday morning, about seven. Roman Osipovich, who had another article to deliver, left the apartment with me. As always, we waited in the hallway for Hannele to shoot the bolt on the latch before we went downstairs.

"What's the article about?" I asked him.

"It's an attack on Bernsteinism," he said. "And right to the point, too."

"Which is?"

I never found out. We'd reached the street. Roman Osipovich made a dash for the downtown trolley, and I walked north for four blocks to a non-kosher butcher shop run by a Polish Jew. He had two barrels of slaughtered chickens, kept in cold storage, which were now thawing out. They were cheap at ten cents a pound.

"Give me a four-pounder," I said.

"This one's four and a half," he said, over the plucked carcass on the scale.

"That's no good. I can only spend forty cents."

"You can have it," he said. "For luck. My first sale of the day."

"It doesn't smell so good to me."

"Nonsense," he said, laying it on the chopping block. He cut open the stomach with a butcher knife and pulled out the guts. The stench bowled me over. I almost puked.

"Never mind, boychik," the butcher said. "We'll find you another one."

He reached into the barrel again. "How's this?"

"It smells okay," I said. "How much does it weigh?"

"Four and a quarter on the nose," he said. "Yours for forty cents."

"Clean it and I'll take it," I said. "But hurry up."

The entrails from the first were on the floor. The stench still nauseated me. "Hurry it up," I told him. He wrapped the gutted carcass in a newspaper and I gave him the forty cents. I drank a glass of seltzer next door and strolled down Houston Street to the Bowery, and back again. It was a muggy, overcast day. The water from the thawed chicken under my arm soaked through the newspaper.

I got home close to ten. The door of the apartment was wide open. Roman Osipovich, coming out of the parlor, said, "She's gone. She went away with Schlifka."

"How do you know?"

"Mrs. Mendel here saw them leave. She lives next door."

The little old woman behind him cupped her hand behind her ear and said, "What's that?"

"Tell him what you saw," Roman Osipovich said in a louder voice.

"Nothing," she said. "I told you. My hearing isn't so good any more."

He shouted into her right ear, "Tell him what you saw."

"Oh," she said. "Yes. I've got eyes like a hawk. About an hour ago, when I opened my door to take out the garbage, I saw a young lady leave here with a man."

"What did he look like?" I asked.

"What's that?"

"Did he have red hair?" I shouted.

"Red hair," she repeated. "Yes, I noticed that."

"What else?"

"He had a walking stick."

"No, I meant . . . What about the girl?"

"What about her?" she repeated. "She was very quiet. She held him by the arm."

"Thank you, Mrs. Mendel," Roman Osipovich said.

"Is there anything wrong?" she asked.

"No, nothing. Thank you very much."

He waited until she'd closed the front door behind her before he said, "That was wide open . . . off the latch . . . when I arrived. Which means only one thing. Hannele let him in. He must have known she was here for a couple of days. Maybe more. He watched us and waited. Then, when she was all alone this morning, he made his move. He knocked on the door, she let him in. They talked—they must have talked—then she went with him quietly, holding his arm."

"What about that?" I asked.

"What?"

"The table in the parlor. Someone turned it over. Your papers are all over the floor."

"Yes," he said. "That's true. I don't know . . . It's possible she had second thoughts and put up a fight. But in the end, when they left . . . you heard the old woman . . . Hannele was holding him by the arm. How can you explain that?"

"I can't."

"What's that you've got there?"

"A chicken. I bought it for us to have tonight. It cost me forty cents."

He took off his pince-nez and rubbed them on his sleeve. "Do you know, I thought . . ." He burst out laughing. "Deep down, I thought of her as a Jewish Sonya. Can you imagine?"

"Who's Sonya?"

"A character in a Russian novel who's a whore."

"What happens to her?"

"In the end, she redeems herself."

"How?"

"Through suffering," he said. "How else? Just like in all Russian novels. She follows her lover into exile in Siberia."

"Is he a Social Democrat?"

"No, a murderer," he said. "He killed two old women with an ax."

"I don't see the connection."

He burst out laughing again. "There isn't any. That's the point."

He clipped his pince-nez back on—he always raised his eyebrows when he did that—and went into the parlor. The heavy table, on a center pedestal, was on its side; the high-backed chair behind it was shoved back against the wall. He knelt down on one knee and began picking up the papers scattered on the floor.

"I didn't love her, you know," he said. "I was attracted to her, of course—she's very pretty—but I didn't love her. And I never touched her, either. I was afraid that after . . ." He stood up. "I felt sorry for her."

"So did I."

"But I should have known better," he said. "It's something I should have learned by now. I can't afford to feel sorry for anyone, ever, including myself."

"Why not?"

"In my profession, it's not allowed."

He sat down on the divan, covered with faded brocade, and glanced at one of the papers in his right hand. " 'The arming of the masses is of the greatest importance,' " he read aloud.

I righted the table.

He crumpled the paper up. "That whore," he said.

I left the chicken, still wrapped in the wet newspaper, on the kitchen table—there was no ice in the icebox—got my valise from under the cot in the hallway, and poked my head in the parlor. Roman Osipovich was sitting at the table with a blank sheet of paper before him and a fountain pen in his hand. The pen had a gold nib.

"I'll be going now," I said. "Thanks for everything."

"Going? Going where?"

"Back to Orchard Street. Feibush might be able to come up with something."

"Feibush? What can Feibush do?" His voice rose. Through the open window behind him there was the prolonged honk of a car horn, which got louder, too, and then died away.

"Whatever he can," I said. "He won't be scared to take Schlifka on."

"Is that what you think?" he asked. "Do you think I'm afraid of Schlifka?"

"I don't know."

He screwed on the top of his fountain pen. "No," he said. "I'm not afraid. I'm apprehensive about getting into trouble with the police, I admit that. If something happens and I get arrested, then all of my work—maybe my life—will be wasted. Useless. For nothing. Yes," he said. "I'm worried about that. But scared of Schlifka? Listen to me.

"In Petersburg, in 1905, on the evening of December 3, the Soviet was surrounded by troops with artillery. All the doors were blocked. We were trapped. The Executive Committee decided 'No resistance, but no arms to be surrendered.'

"We only had revolvers. I had a Mauser, which I kept in a wooden holster. I looked out the window.

There, in the snow, was a detachment of cavalry—Ural Cossacks in long overcoats—with their sabers drawn, held up against their right shoulders. Here and there a blade flashed in the light. Once in the beam of an acetylene searchlight mounted on an open touring car, a Mercedes, with an officer in the back . . .

"All around me, in the meeting hall, the workers were following their orders. I, too, did as I was told. I smashed my Mauser against a Browning. The trigger broke off. The bullets in the pocket of my leather jacket, eight of them, were useless. I threw them and the wooden holster on the floor. I was defenseless, like all the others. But afraid?" He shook his head.

"No," he said. "A pimp doesn't scare me." He laughed. "Anyway, as I've told you, to be a Marxist is to be something of a fatalist. If I get into trouble with the police over this, then . . ." He shrugged. "Did you have anything specific in mind?"

"I don't know," I said. "I was thinking . . . I can't do it, Schlifka and the girls know me. But you or Feibush can get into the whorehouse as a customer, take care of Schlifka, and bring Hannele out. It'll only cost you two bucks."

"As a customer?"

"It's first come, first served, but if you buy a drink for another buck, you can hang around the parlor and take your pick as the girls come out. As soon as you spot Hannele, grab her and make a run for it."

"Supposing she's not there?"

"In that case, I guess, you'll have to pick out one of the other girls, go to her room, and find out where Hannele is. Judy, for example. No, that's no good.

She's a shiksa from Corning, New York, who speaks only English. You'll have to talk with one of the others. There's one—I forget her name—who has a rash. She speaks Yiddish, as I remember."

"A rash? What kind of a rash? Where?"

"On her neck, in the back, and on the inside of her arm."

"Anywhere else?"

"I don't know."

"I don't like the sound of it," he said.

"All you have to do is talk with her. Slip her an extra buck."

"I can't," he said. "I have only three dollars to my name."

"Give her this."

He stuck my dollar bill in his pocket and said, "This is against my principles."

"There's one other thing."

"What's that?" he asked.

"You'll have to take off your spats."

"My spats? Why?"

"I once mentioned to Schlifka that you wore them."

"Oh, you did, did you?"

"Just in passing."

"Well, it makes no difference now. He must already know what I look like."

"I never thought of that."

"I'll have to take my chances."

"Does that mean you'll do it?"

"Yes," he said. "But on one condition."

"Anything."

"You stay out of it."

"You'll need all the help you can get."

"It's up to you. Make up your mind."

"Okay, it's a deal."

"Is that a promise?"

"Yes," I said. "I swear. When do we go?"

"The sooner the better, if you ask me."

"Tonight?"

"Yes, tonight," he said.

He was in there almost half an hour. I waited for him on the stairs and in the hallway of the floor below. The shoemaker, coming home from shul in a black suit, wished me "Good Shabbes."

"Yes, and to you, too, Grandpa," I said. "To you and yours."

Beside his door a big chunk of plaster had flaked from the wall; the sheet rock underneath, riddled with holes, looked like worm-eaten wood which had been turned to stone. It was shiny and damp. I sat down on the bottom step. There was the smell of freshly baked bread. Above me, a door opened, and Yetta said, "You're welcome any time. Come and see us again."

"I will," Roman Osipovich told her.

"Well?"

"I was right. She's not there."

Because of Shabbes, the street was almost empty. There were candles burning in some of the ground-floor apartments. On one table was a silver kiddush cup; at another I could make out all the people: a man in a black bowler, two kids with shaved heads wearing payess, a fat woman.

"The one with the rash—her name is Sophie—speaks Yiddish, all right, but I couldn't . . . I talked with Rosa, instead," Roman Osipovich said. "The one on morphine, six or eight grains a day. Schlifka addicted her. She's into him for six or seven hundred dollars, she's not sure, which means she works for nothing. All four of them up there owe him money for their perfume and their clothes—even their hairpins.

"They each earn from forty to fifty dollars a week, but have to give him half. And they're not allowed to handle any cash. Just those brass tokens. Yetta keeps the books, so you can imagine. I offered Rosa the dollar, once we were in her room, but she was too scared to take it. Her voice shook.

" 'No, no, give it to Mama,' she said. 'Tell her to charge it to my account.'

" 'Mama,' I repeated. Then she passed out on the bed, with her eyes open. Did you happen to notice her eyes? The left pupil?"

"What about Hannele?"

"I'm coming to that. She knows that Schlifka has a new girl. She's jealous, if you can believe it. Terribly jealous. He's keeping her somewhere. She overheard him telling Yetta that they'd be back by Friday, at the latest, but she has no idea where they are."

"I do," I said.

"How?"

"Schlifka once showed me the building."

"Then let's go."

"It's on this side of the street," I said. "But I'm not sure which block. Maybe the next."

Five doors down, the sagging black and white tiles on the floor of a hallway were familiar. When I stopped, he asked, "Is this it?"

"Yes, I think so. It's on the second floor. One of the apartments in the back."

We raced up the stairs. The door of the rear apartment on the left was half open. Someone sneezed twice, and a woman called out, "Gesundheit."

"The other one," Roman Osipovich said.

"It's locked."

"Can you hear anything?"

"No."

"Stand back."

A clash of metal behind us made me turn around. A big orange cat had knocked the lid off the garbage can under the stairwell. "Go on, scat," I said, waving my arms, but it stayed where it was, perched on the rim.

Roman Osipovich pounded and yelled, "Open this door."

The cat jumped to the floor. Its eyes glowed.

"Open up," Roman Osipovich yelled.

A kid about my age stuck his head out of the other apartment and said in English, "You're wasting your time. Red ain't there."

"Are you sure?" I asked him.

"He ain't been there for over two weeks. There ain't nobody there now."

"No girl?"

"Nobody."

"What'd he say?" Roman Osipovich asked me.

"They're not there."

"Does he have any idea where they are?"

The kid shook his head and grinned. One of his upper front teeth was black. He called after us down the stairs, "Tough luck," and laughed.

At home, Roman Osipovich asked me, "Are you hungry or do you want to go right to bed?"

"I could eat something."

"Me too," he said. He threw two handfuls of coal from the half-filled scuttle on the floor into the stove. "I'll boil the chicken. There's no sense in letting it go to waste."

"I like it better roasted."

"We haven't any schmaltz."

"I'll borrow some from Mrs. Mendel."

"We need salt, too," he said, taking the cover off the iron pot. Then he added, "This pot is filthy."

"She wasn't much of a housekeeper," I said.

We made the chicken last three days—the time it took me to find a new job as a presser in a shop on Kenmare Street.

"It's only temporary, you understand," the foreman said. "Reisner, my regular, is out sick."

"What's the matter with him?"

"Varicose veins."

"How much does he get?" I asked.

"Seven cents a piece."

"That's okay with me."

"I'll give you six."

"I'll take it," I said.

"When can you start?"

"Right away. I already had lunch."

"That's your spot, there," he told me. "By the window. You're lucky. Sometimes you get a breeze."

Two or three of the other pressers, taking a break, had scattered bread crumbs on the ledge covered with pigeon shit. The birds fluttered and pecked while I worked.

That night Roman Osipovich and I decided to go for a walk after supper. He left the door of the apartment ajar.

"You never know," he said. "She might give him the slip."

"Not Schlifka."

"You can never tell."

"I think she loves him," I said.

"No," he said. "It's not love."

"Then what is it?"

"A lack of self-awareness. It's as if she were asleep. She's not yet conscious of being exploited; not yet, anyway. She must be awakened, you see, just like the masses . . . the whole race. All of them."

He repeated, "All of them," on the sidewalk, where two kids pitched pennies against the stoop and an old woman filled a pail from the open hydrant at the curb.

On Friday morning, as I waited for my irons to get hot, I heard the foreman say, "Well, I don't know. He's young, healthy, and he works cheap."

A man answered, "But you promised me," and I looked up. He was standing at the end of the long wooden table, to my right, with one hand on the head of a sewing machine.

"I've got four mouths to feed," he said.

An operator came between us—she had blond hair

—and the starting bell went off. I looked away. The fifteen or twenty sewing machines in the place rasped and whirred.

I picked up an iron. Then a voice whispered in my left ear, "How much does he pay you?"

"Six cents a piece," I said without turning around.

"He's cheating you. I got eight."

"I'll take what I can get."

"You're taking the bread out of my children's mouths," he said.

The face of the bearded presser on the other side of the stove shimmered in the heated air.

Behind me the foreman said, "Leave him alone, Reisner."

One of them cleared his throat.

"I've got two boys and a girl," Reisner said.

The foreman shouted, "That's enough," and I turned around just in time to see Reisner limp away. He favored his right leg—the one on which a presser always pivoted when he hefted the iron from the stove to the board.

Twenty minutes or so after I got home, Roman Osipovich came out of his room with half a bottle of vodka.

"Are you drunk?" I asked him.

"I've never been drunk in my life."

"Your shirt is wringing wet."

"It's hot in here," he said, putting the bottle on the kitchen table.

"Shall we go?"

"Yes, it's time."

We crossed Canal Street; the gravel in the gutter

crunched under our feet. On the other side a bunch of men were arguing in Italian.

"I saw Sasha this afternoon," Roman Osipovich said. "He's got a room right off Rutgers Park. We can take her there."

"Then what?"

"Then we'll see," he said.

Like the week before, I caught a whiff of freshly baked bread on the second floor of the building on Allen Street.

"You wait down here," Roman Osipovich said.

"Not on your life."

We started up the next flight of stairs. Ahead of us, in the open doorway, there was a Chinaman with a pigtail holding a wicker basket filled with ruffled drawers.

"What about my sheets?" Yetta asked him in English.

"In morning," the Chinaman said. "First thing."

"And what about this?" she asked. "It's scorched."

"Where?"

"Right here. You ruined the lace."

"Get out of my way," Roman Osipovich said.

Yetta called out, "Red!" and tried to slam the door in his face. The wicker basket, dropped on its side, got in the way. Roman Osipovich kicked the door open. The Chinaman, on his hands and knees, scrambled to pick the laundry up from the floor. In one hand, against his chest, he clutched the drawers with the scorched lace. I stepped over him. Roman Osipovich was in the middle of the parlor. Yetta called out, "Red!" again, and a girl jumped up from the wooden bench. In the opposite corner, Schlifka was lighting a cigar above the chimney of the lamp on the table.

"So you're the Social Democrat," he said.

"Yes."

"The worker."

"That's right."

Schlifka laughed. "Well, I can't talk." He puffed on the cigar. "What do you want?"

"Where's Hannele?"

"There's a hard worker for you," Schlifka said. "She's working now." He looked at me for the first time and asked in English, "Are you a Social Democrat, too?"

"I don't know."

"You're much too smart for that."

He stuck out his right hand and Yetta gave him his walking stick. "Now get out of here," he said in Yiddish. "Both of you."

"Where's Hannele?" Roman Osipovich repeated.

"You really want to see her, do you? Sure, why not?" He asked Yetta, "Which room is she in?"

"The first one on the left."

"Be my guest," Schlifka said.

I opened the door. Hannele was on her back in bed, naked, with her legs wrapped around some guy with a hairy ass.

"Happy now?" Schlifka asked.

Roman Osipovich grabbed him around the neck with both hands. The cigar fell out of his mouth. They staggered back four or five feet into the parlor again, where Schlifka caught a high heel on one of those burlap sacks nailed to the floor and tripped. Roman Osipovich, who didn't let go, landed on top of him. The pince-nez stayed on his nose.

Then Schlifka jabbed him in the ribs with the end of his stick. They rolled over, toward the bench. Schlifka jabbed him again. The next thing I knew, they were apart, on the floor, and a second after that up on their feet, facing each other.

Hannele was in the entrance to the hallway; her nipples were rouged. She wiped off the bush between her legs with the corner of a wet towel and asked, "What's going on?"

"It's your boy friend," Schlifka said. "The Social Democrat. He wants to see you."

"He can do anything he wants with me for two bucks," she said.

"You hear that?" Schlifka asked Roman Osipovich.

"I hear," he said.

"That's cheap at the price."

"That goes for the kid, too," Hannele said. "Any time."

"How would you like that?" Schlifka asked, without looking at me.

"No."

"Don't you like me?" Hannele asked.

"Yes," I said. "I like you very much."

"Then come and fuck me."

"No."

"Leave him alone," Roman Osipovich said.

"You come, too. I'll fuck you both at once."

Schlifka laughed and raised his stick in both hands above his head. The gold handle cast a shadow on the low ceiling. Roman Osipovich stepped back.

"He doesn't want you either," Schlifka said.

"So it seems."

"Spread your legs and give him a good look."

"I already have."

"Do it again with your fingers," Schlifka said. "No, it's no use. He's not interested. What should I do with him?"

"Whatever you like."

"I could cripple him," he said.

The shadow moved along the ceiling. Roman Osipovich took another step back. Hannele brushed the hair from her eyes; they were half closed. The stick came down.

"Stand still," Schlifka yelled.

Roman Osipovich, who had jumped to the left, had one hand on the floor; the other was clenched. Schlifka raised the stick again.

"Kill him," Hannele whispered. "Kill him for me. Oh, kill him for me now with that stick."

I screamed, and Schlifka glanced at me. Roman Osipovich kicked him in the balls and, when he was doubled over, brought up his hands, which were clasped together, and caught him in the throat. Schlifka hit his head on the edge of the bench going down. I hauled off to kick him, too, but he cracked me on the right shin, just below the knee, with the handle of the stick. I rolled on the floor.

I'm fuzzy about what happened next. I think Roman Osipovich kicked Schlifka again—in the jaw or ear, I wasn't sure which—and he groaned. Yetta made a grab for the stick. I can see her bending over; her necklace swung back and forth.

"Stay where you are," Roman Osipovich said. "Don't move."

I shut my eyes. Then I remember Hannele opening the front door. She was wearing her red dress; it was unbuttoned at the neck.

"Where are you going?" Roman Osipovich asked her.

"I didn't mean it," she said.

"I know that."

Yetta, who picked up the laundry basket, laughed, and Hannele ran out.

Roman Osipovich shouted after her, "Wait, for God's sake."

She screamed in the hallway, "I meant every word," and I heard her scream again from the stairs.

Roman Osipovich picked up the stick and examined the gold handle. "What do you know? It's the head of a dog; one with pointed ears." He hefted the stick in his hands. "Heavy. What kind of wood is it? Ebony?" he asked Schlifka. He raised his chin; the brilliantine had kept his hair slicked down; it was still parted in the middle. There was blood oozing from his left ear; it was all over his rubber collar. Roman Osipovich leaned the walking stick at an angle against the wall by the door and stomped on it; it broke in half.

"Can you stand up?" he asked me.

"I can try."

"Put your arm around my neck."

Halfway down the stairs, I gagged, but couldn't bring anything up.

"Your leg is bleeding," Roman Osipovich said.

"Is it really? I didn't know."

"That's all right. I'll take you to Miriam Tauber's. She'll fix you up."

"You'd better go after Hannele."

"I will, right afterward," he said. "She'll be back at the apartment."

"How do you know?"

"I just do. It's a feeling. I've had it all night."

"She won't be able to get in."

"Yes, she will," he said. "I left the door open when we left. Didn't you notice?"

"No," I said. "I can't say that I did."

10

MRS. TAUBER SAID, "The cloth is stuck to the cut. I'll have to pull it off."

"Then go ahead," I told her.

"There," she said. "How's that?"

"Not too bad."

"It's bleeding again. Take off your pants. I want to take a look."

"I can't."

"Why not?"

"I'm not wearing any underwear."

Feibush tossed her a folded quilt. "Here, cover him up with that," he said.

I lay back on the davenport with my leg on her lap, while she washed out the cut with soap and water from a basin. I was cut to the bone; my shin was swollen and purple.

"I don't feel anything," I said. "It's completely numb."

"Not for long. I think you ought to have it stitched up."

"No, that'll heal by itself," Feibush said.

"Bring me a clean sheet and tear off a couple of strips," she told him.

Ten or fifteen minutes later, in the middle of my story, the leg began to throb. "I think the bandage is too tight," I said.

"No, leave it alone."

"What happened next?" Feibush asked.

"Schlifka said, 'Use your fingers,' and she dropped the wet towel and did. She winked at Roman Osipovich with the eye that has the mole. And then she winked at me."

"And after that?"

It took me another ten minutes to tell them the rest. Mrs. Tauber put out her cigarette in the basin of bloody water, and Feibush rubbed his chin. I yawned.

"Get yourself some sleep," he said.

"Yes, I could use some."

Later on, through the closed door, I heard Roman Osipovich's voice, and I raised my head from the pillow and said, "Wait for me. I'll come, too."

I left the window open. One of those white pigeons, cooing on the fire escape, woke me up. It was light. With the quilt around me, I limped into the kitchen where Feibush and Mrs. Tauber were having coffee. Her hair was tangled, and she was wearing the same rumpled dress—the blue-and-white-striped gingham—as the night before.

"How's the leg?" she asked me.

"Sore."

Feibush said, "Hannele's dead. She killed herself last night."

I leaned on the table and asked, "How?"

"With the gas in the kitchen, as soon as she got back to Roman Osipovich's apartment. Some old lady who lives next door smelled it and tried to save her, but it was too late."

"Mrs. Mendel?"

"I didn't catch her name," he said. "She had trouble opening the door because Hannele had stuffed a woolen blanket under it. By the time she got it open, Roman Osipovich had arrived. Hannele was on the floor, next to a chair, right under the jet; the glass mantle was on the table. My guess is that she took it off, got up on the chair, stuck the jet in her mouth, probably holding her nose, and breathed in the gas until she passed out or died. There was nothing Roman Osipovich could do. He came over here."

"I thought I dreamed it."

"We all went back there with her papa and Ostrovsky at about five," he said. "Before we left, I told the old man the whole story."

"Everything?"

"I had to. He insisted on it."

"What'd he say?"

"Nothing. He listened without a word. We went downstairs. The sun was coming up. Then he turned around and went back to his apartment for a minute

—I was with him—and he put a little pair of scissors, a bottle of white wine, and a comb in a paper bag, which he brought along. On Centre Street, he bought an egg. Ostrovsky took him aside in a doorway, but I couldn't hear what he said. The old man played with his beard and then whispered in his ear for a good five minutes, maybe more. Outside the house Ostrovsky grabbed his sleeve, but the old man shook him off and said, 'No, the time has come.' "

"Meaning what?"

"I've no idea."

"We can't get the body away from him," Mrs. Tauber said. "He took off all her clothes. She was already stiff as a board. In the end, he ripped the dress off and stood her up on her feet against the wall, next to the divan in the parlor. He said, 'We ought to have some straw for the floor.' Then he poured warm water over her head six or eight times, from an iron pot he heated up on the stove. He kept going back to the kitchen for more. Finally, when she was soaking wet and there was a big puddle on the floor, he washed her all over with his hand—even between her toes—and dried her off with a woolen blanket.

"After that, he laid her down on the divan again, on her back, and in the same saucepan mixed the wine and the egg—the shell, too—and bathed her head with it. Then he combed out her hair very carefully, and cut the ends with those little scissors from the paper bag. He also tore off a strip from the hem of her dress and tied up her jaw with it. That was the first thing he did, as a matter of fact.

"Her mouth was wide open, just like Tofetsky. She's the same color, too. Bright red. I imagine that's from the gas, don't you?" Then she added, "That old man won't listen to reason."

"Let me go and have a talk with him," I said.

"It won't do any good."

"Let me try."

"He asked after you," Feibush said.

"Yes, that's true, he did," Mrs. Tauber said. "But you've got nothing to wear. I washed your pants last night. They're still wet."

"I'll lend him my brown ones," Feibush said.

When we arrived, the old man was brushing a handful of nail parings into a handkerchief spread on the parlor table.

"I heard what you did," he said. "You're a good boy."

"And what you're doing is forbidden," I told him.

"No, not any more."

"At least let me cover her up," Roman Osipovich said.

The corpse, stretched out on the brocade divan, was still bright red. The scalp, under the wet hair combed back behind the ears, was the same color as the rag tied under the jaw.

"No," he repeated. "The time has come for us, at last, to break all of our holy Laws, one by one. Are you surprised? Well, so was I. It came to me this morning on the street, as the sun came up. All of a sudden, after all these years, I understood. So will you. You know what we're taught in the *Midrash Tehillim.* We've discussed it."

"What does it say there?" Roman Osipovich asked him.

"Do you know the holy tongue?"

"Not a word."

"Ah, then, in Yiddish, it goes: 'Israel speaks to God: When will you redeem us? And He answers: When you have sunk to the lowest level, at that time will I redeem you.' Now do you understand?" he asked me. " 'The lowest level' . . ."

Ostrovsky said, "The rabbi thinks . . . He believes that the time is ripe for us to descend to the lower spheres through the Gates of Impurity, as we say, to the realm of the *kelipot.*"

"The what?" Roman Osipovich asked.

"It's hard to explain," Ostrovsky said. "It means . . . We must break open all the shells, everywhere, in order to raise up the divine sparks . . . to restore them . . ."

"What does that mean?" Roman Osipovich asked.

"He believes we can force the End and bring the Messiah."

"The Messiah? But that's crazy."

"I know it," Ostrovsky said.

The old man spoke to me again. "We can hasten it, if we try. We must. It's worth it, for even one day . . . a single hour. Even so, it'll take years and years. First will come the War of Gog and Magog, the End of Days, but then . . . Who knows? You might live to see the rest: all the sparks restored, the Exile ended, death swallowed up. The Temple, you know, will be rebuilt, and the divine lovers will embrace again in the Holy of Holies, face to face. The King and His bride, who is also called the Shekinah, the Matronit, and Earth. Do you know about that?"

"No."

"Ah, but you should. You might live long enough to dance at the wedding. Yes, that's possible. You're going to live a long time."

"I am?"

He looked at Roman Osipovich. "And you're going to die in Russia," he said.

"I hope so."

"Your own brother will kill you."

"I haven't got a brother."

"No? Then someone—I don't know who—wearing a blue cap. You'll be old, too. Or at least gray. All gray, with a little pointed beard. But he—the one in the blue cap—will be much younger than that."

"And how will he do it?" Roman Osipovich asked.

"You already know how," the old man said. "It'll happen in a root cellar . . . No, a basement. A room in a basement, with white tiles on the walls and something . . . a canvas, I think . . . Yes, a canvas on the floor. They'll strip you to your underwear—long woolen underwear—with drawstrings around the ankles."

"You're right about one thing, old man," Roman Osipovich said.

"Oh? What's that?"

"We must force the End."

"Did anyone call the police?" Mrs. Tauber asked.

"The old lady next door," Feibush said. "They should have been here by now."

"Hand me the blanket. I'm going to cover her up."

Bent over the table, the old man poked his finger through the nail parings, tied the ends of the handkerchief together, and stuck it in his pocket. Then he stared out the window.

"What can I use for the floor?" Mrs. Tauber asked Roman Osipovich. "Have you got a mop?"

"I'll get you a rag from the kitchen."

She was on her hands and knees when the cop on the beat finally arrived. He lifted one end of the blanket, let it drop, and said, "The meat wagon's on the way."

"The meat wagon?" I repeated.

"The wagon from the morgue."

Mrs. Tauber squeezed the wet rag into the saucepan and stood up.

"Who're you?" he asked her.

"I'm the only one here who speaks English," I said.

"Well, give it to me slow and easy," he said, taking out a pad and pencil. "Names and addresses first."

He was left-handed and wrote very slowly; in the middle of everything, he took off his white helmet and wiped the sweat from his forehead with his sleeve. "Okay," he told me. "Keep going."

"That's all I know," I said. "She was out of work, and her father is very sick."

"What's the matter with him?"

"What do you think?"

"He's crazy."

"You guessed it."

"Yeah, I noticed the way he stares out the window. He ain't moved a muscle since I came in. What about what's-his-name? The guy behind the chair."

"He and Hannele were friends."

"That's all?"

"As far as I know."

"But this is his place, ain't it?"

"Yeah."

"That's what I thought," he said, turning a page. "Who took off all her clothes?"

"She did, before she turned on the gas."

"Not according to the old lady next door. She told me she found the body fully dressed." He leafed back through his notes. "She was wearing a red dress. Just like that one over there on the floor."

"Well, the old lady's got it wrong."

"How do you know? Was you here when it happened?"

"No."

He tapped his pencil against a tooth. "But neither was her boy friend."

"That's true," I said. "He got here right after she died."

"But, according to the old lady, he carried the body in here from the kitchen and was alone with it for ten or fifteen minutes."

"That I couldn't say."

"I'd like to have a little chat with this guy," he said.

"Right this minute?"

"Tomorrow or the next day will do. There's no rush." He turned another page and scribbled again with his left hand on the pad. "This here's the address of my precinct, along with my name. I'm there every night after eight."

"I'll tell him," I said.

"What's he speak, anyhow?"

"Yiddish and Russian."

"That's okay. I'll get Nathanson to translate," he said.

There was a clanging in the street. "That's the meat wagon now."

"Is there anything else you want from me?" I asked.

"No," he said. "You can go."

Feibush lugged my valise back to Mrs. Tauber's. It was almost noon. I decided to get out of town as fast as I could.

11

I SNEAKED OUT the next morning, just before dawn, without saying goodbye. At Christopher Street I caught the ferry to Hoboken and then grabbed the first train out. It was the Delaware, Lackawanna and Western. A ticket to Buffalo cost two bucks. That left me nine dollars and sixty cents.

The train went through Paterson, a big town. The factories, made of red brick, were blackened by soot; it covered up the windows as well. Then we were out in the open under a cloudy sky, chugging past the Denville station, with its gabled roof, and into the Delaware Water Gap. The train and the river ran side by side for almost two miles at the bottom of a gorge. There was a small steamer on the water; I could make out an awning on the deck and a man in a white suit leaning over the rail. The sun came out. We stopped at Scranton; I didn't like the look of it.

At Binghamton, though, just for the hell of it, I got off to try my luck. A Jew by the name of Borowitz, who owned the dry-goods store opposite the Bennett Hotel, gave me a job sweeping up. All I had to do was walk in off the street and speak Yiddish to him.

He was from Bendery, near Kishinev, and had come over right after the pogrom in 1903.

"We had the Black Hundreds in Bendery, too," he said. "I knew it was only a matter of time."

I slept on a canvas cot in the back. In the mornings, at six-thirty, I opened up for business. There was a cracked tin bell on the door, which got on my nerves. So did Borowitz and his wife. They never stopped asking me questions.

Also, my leg hurt. After about a week my ankle turned purple and swelled up. I thought I was in for trouble, but then the pain stopped, and one night, when I took off the bandage, I saw that the cut had a scab. Two days after that, I caught the milk train to Elmira. It was a Wednesday, I remember; Rosh Hashanah began that night.

This time I tried my luck at a coalyard on Main Street owned by a Jew named Weiss.

"Do you know anything about working in a coalyard?" he asked me.

"Nothing."

"So you'll learn," he said in English. His Yiddish was a little rusty; it improved as the morning went on —we talked in his office for almost two hours—but I had a hard time with his accent. He was a Litvak from a town called Panevicz, which had an important yeshiva. He'd been in America since 1886. Why Elmira? His father's older brother was there. Three weeks after he and his parents arrived, his father died of a heart attack. After a couple of months, it was obvious that the brother didn't want to be saddled with a woman and a kid. He ran out on them, probably to New York.

With seven dollars left between them, Weiss and his mother took a room over the barber shop on Main Street and bought about five dollars' worth from Lyton's, the big dry-goods store up the block. It was the middle of winter. The two of them tied rags around their shoes and loaded up. They peddled denim, shoelaces, potato mashers, and pots and pans to the farmers on Big Flats. "The first time out, we made a profit of three bucks," Weiss said.

Muma Leah, as his mother was called, was still alive at seventy-six. She quit work in 1891, when they'd scraped up enough to buy a horse and wagon. Five years later, with a loan from a farmer who also owned a lot of land on East Hills, Weiss bought the coalyard; the anthracite was shipped from Scranton. He married his second cousin, whom he brought over from Panevicz in the summer of 1896. They had two daughters, who were now fourteen and sixteen years old.

"Mrs. Weiss died three years ago," he said. "In October, may she rest in peace."

"I'm sorry. That can't be easy."

"Or for you, either," he said. "All alone, at your age."

"What makes you say that?"

"Why else is a Jewish kid your age looking for a job on yontif in Elmira, New York?"

He took me home for lunch to his white clapboard house on Lake Street. In the dining room, he put on a yarmulke, washed his hands in a glass bowl, and recited the benediction before we sat down. I met his older daughter, Mildred, who cut me dead; Sylvia was at school. The old lady, who wore a black wig, watched me like a hawk.

The rest of the afternoon I spent hanging around the coalyard. At about four-thirty Weiss said, "We quit early today because of yontif. You can come to shul with us, if you like."

"No, thank you."

"Suit yourself," he said.

He put me up on a cot in his attic.

The four of them went to services again after breakfast the next morning, and again I stayed around the house. There was a player piano in the parlor; I'd never seen one before. It was a cinch to work. I listened over and over to a song by Victor Herbert called "Baghdad." It started pouring. I closed the window in the kitchen, where the curtain was already sopped.

As they came in, at about twelve-thirty, Mildred asked her father, "But why do we blow the shofar on Rosh Hashanah?"

"For two reasons," I said, and she looked at me for the first time. "You'd better take off your coat first. You'll catch your death."

"Jake's right. Go in the parlor and dry off by the fire," her father said, leaving his dripping umbrella open and upside down on the floor by the door. I blew on the white coals in the big, fancy Sunburst stove; it had a nickel dome.

"Well? What are they?" Mildred asked me again.

"It's supposed to remind us of the Akedah and the coming of the Messiah."

"What's the Akedah again? I forget."

"The Binding of Isaac," her father explained.

"I don't get it," she said to me. "What's the connection between them?"

"Farfetched."

"Don't you believe in God?"

"I don't believe in any of those promises," I said. "No future will redeem us; not with the human heart."

Sylvia piped up, "What's wrong with the human heart?"

"I wish I knew."

Weiss paid me two and a half dollars a week, plus room and board. In a couple of months, he raised it to three. I helped Ed Cory, who'd worked in the yard for six years; we made deliveries in the big wagon, which was famous in Elmira. It was painted dark green; the spokes of the wheels were red. There was a sheepskin spread on the seat.

The first thing I learned was how to hitch up the two big black geldings, a matched pair. I still know all the parts of an Eastern harness: the bridles, the lines, the wooden hames, bound in iron, the breast straps, the traces, the breechings and the martingales, with rings in the loops. The trimmings were brass.

Cory handled the reins; the brake was between us

on the floor, near his right foot. My job was to hose the coal down after it was loaded and weighed, then to ride along and give Cory a hand with a scoop. Most of the houses in town had coal sheds; six or eight of the bigger ones—over near City Hall—had furnaces in the basement; that meant shoveling the coal through a window down a steel chute. I had to tie a kerchief over my nose and mouth because of the dust.

Once in a while, when we finished, the lady of the house gave us a drink of lemonade or whiskey; after the first snow, at the end of November, we brought our own bottle along.

That was around the time I discovered that Weiss gave free coal to the Herzogs, another Jewish family in town. They were Litvaks from Vilna who lived in a two-family house on Church Street. The shed in the alley had burned down; we had to pile the coal in the open, outside the back door. The dust, blown across the yard, turned the snow black. Mrs. Herzog carried a scuttle at a time inside; she was always complaining about her back. Her husband was a man of fifty or so who'd gone broke in the clothing business—a men's shop—five or six years before. He worked as a grocery clerk at Cutter's on Water Street. Cory told me that Weiss gave him free coal every winter, all winter long.

"But that's a secret, you understand," he said. "The boss don't want nobody to know. Specially Miss Mildred. He thinks she's snotty enough as it is."

It got very cold and there was a lot of snow. I had to spend three twenty-five for buckskin gloves and a pair of gum boots lined with felt. My attic wasn't heated, so I spent the evenings with the family downstairs. We sat around the parlor stove. I didn't talk much. I couldn't take my eyes off Mildred, particularly the nape of her neck. She wore her hair up. It was auburn, like Mrs. Tauber's. Once or twice, bent over some sewing, she stared back at me; otherwise she never gave me a tumble.

Her sister, Sylvia, on the other hand, had the hots for me ever since that first night. She was always trying to start up a conversation. Finally one evening right after the first of the year, she said, "You're not very friendly, you know. Sometimes you're downright rude."

"I'm sorry," I told her. "I don't mean to be."

"I'll forgive you if you take me for a walk."

"Done."

In the deep snow, which reached my knees, we got as far as the big oak tree on the corner before she ran out of breath and stopped. The branches, covered with ice, squeaked in the wind.

"Just look at the way the full moon blots out all those stars," she said. "Do you know any of the constellations? That's Orion, up there, toward the southwest; those three stars in a row. See it? Our teacher, Miss Godwin, says that when you look at the stars, you're looking into the distant past."

"Why is that?"

"They're very far away . . . millions and millions of miles . . . and so it takes millions and millions of years for their light to reach us. That makes me happy to be alive right now, doesn't it you?"

"I guess so."

"Right this second," she said. "Which is already gone."

Muma Leah, who had a cataract in one eye, didn't trust me. She kept her bedroom door locked when I was around. Sylvia told me not to take it personally. "She's a little cracked," she said.

The old lady had a strongbox stuffed with cash hidden somewhere in her room. She sold the presents they gave her.

At dinner, Sylvia asked, "How much did you get from Mrs. Mills for that watch Papa got you on your birthday, Grandma?"

The old lady's face was reflected in the oval mirror with beveled edges on the sideboard; she had no teeth. "Not enough," she answered in Yiddish.

In the middle of February, Weiss—like my father—celebrated the holiday *Chamishoh Oser Bi Sh'vot.* It's supposed to be the day when the sap begins to rise in the fruit trees that grow in the Holy Land.

The night before, we stuffed ourselves on almonds, figs, and apples. I brought up the bowl of apples from the cellar; the cold, the wooden bin, and the dirt floor kept them pretty fresh.

Weiss put on his yarmulke, opened his Bible on the dining-room table, and, according to the custom, read aloud from certain parts of Genesis, Leviticus, Deuteronomy, and Ezekiel. The old lady was asleep in her rocking chair. The girls, who didn't understand Hebrew, munched on the apples; I ate almost all the figs. He wound up with the end of the Psalm,

> The pastures are clothed with flocks; the valleys also are covered over with corn; they shout for joy, they also sing.

That put a bug in my head, but the sachet was stale. The next morning, slogging through the snow on our way to the yard, I asked Weiss for Friday off.

"I want to see a couple of friends of mine in New York," I said.

He told me, "Why not? Take Sunday, too."

12

THE OVEN WAS LIT, but I could still see my own breath. Feibush, who was sitting next to me, rubbed his red hands together and blew between them.

Mrs. Tauber said, "I'm due early in July."

"Mazeltov."

"Thank you."

"Are you still working?"

"Why not? I feel fine. Besides, we need the money. I'll keep at it as long as I can."

"It's not easy for her," Feibush said. "She's got a bad case of piles, and by the end of the day her ankles are all swelled up."

"It's nothing," she said. "It'll pass."

"She has nosebleeds, too."

"That's just from the cold weather. It doesn't mean a thing."

"What do you do for the piles?" I asked her.

She laughed. "Sit on this pillow all day. I take it to work with me."

"And what about you?" I asked Feibush. "How's your work going?"

"So-so. Winter's not the best time for a carpenter. The last job I had was a week and a half ago. I put in new doors at the Windsor. The manager gave me two tickets for the show. We saw *Broken Chains,* by Kobrin; a revival. Not bad," he said. "All in all, we can't complain."

"Neither can I."

"I'm glad to hear it," Mrs. Tauber said.

"Have you seen Roman Osipovich lately?"

"He disappeared the next day, the same as you."

"I'm not surprised."

"He arranged the funeral, though, for nothing, through the Workmen's Circle. She's buried at Mount Carmel, in Brooklyn."

"What about the old man?" I asked. "How's he?"

"On his last legs," Feibush said. "Ostrovsky took him in. We give what we can. Not that he needs much. He eats once a day, in the mornings; a little groats boiled in milk. The rest of the time he stays in bed, all bundled up in a goose-feather quilt, with a book open on his lap. He only gets up to go to the toilet, which is more and more frequent. He's got bladder trouble but won't use a chamber pot. I don't know why."

Mrs. Tauber said, "He married us, you know. He insisted on it; he begged us, so we gave in."

"When was this?"

"The night of September 23. He refused to wait until he was out of mourning; the Thirty Days. He made a scene about it; something terrible. But he was very calm at the ceremony—very dignified. He wore a white silk caftan; Ostrovsky borrowed it for him.

"We had it here, in the parlor, under a rented chupah; an embroidered one with a fringe. We got it for a dollar at Singer and Lehmann's, on East Broadway. The schnapps, too, at half the price. Singer's brother is in the liquor business. It was a nice party. We missed you. Riegler, my boss, was here with his wife; they're back together again."

"You haven't asked about Schlifka," Feibush said.

"What about him?"

"There's a rumor in the neighborhood that he's deaf in one ear."

Mrs. Tauber, who'd slipped one hand under her coat, said, "It's kicking. There it goes again. Sometimes you can feel the head and either an elbow or a knee; it's hard to tell which. This is the head, right here. Would you like to feel it?" she asked me.

"Very much."

"Then come over here and give me your hand. Don't be afraid. Just put your palm right here. That's it. Now wait. There," she said. "Did you feel that?"

"It's wonderful."

We talked until two in the morning; a slice of lemon in some tea, left on the sink, froze to the bottom of the glass. I wore my sheepskin coat over my clothes in bed.

There was a roaring fire under the iron kettle; sparks and black smoke rose in the air. The bucket was overturned. Nikodomich, who was standing beside me, asked in Yiddish, "Do you smell those roses?"

"Yes. And violets, too."

"That means she's on the way; our Moist Mother Earth."

The bone handle of his knife was sticking out of the top of his right boot. He was wearing a linen blouse over his pants. There was a rope tied around his waist; the frayed ends dangled between his legs.

"She's here," he whispered.

A log rolled out of the fire. Mrs. Tauber dumped an armful of straw next to the bucket. Her red dress was hitched up over her belly, showing her thighs. The seam was split under her left arm. She had on a necklace of silver coins. The smoldering log gave off a few sparks. Nikodomich dropped to his knees, with his arms outstretched, and pressed his forehead against the ground, near a stone.

"Get down," he told me. "You're not allowed to watch."

"I'm the father."

"Are you sure?"

"Yes."

"Then you have to watch everything."

The bright sky was very hazy; I couldn't find the sun.

"What's she doing now?" Nikodomich whispered.

"I've no idea."

"You have to watch."

"She broke water all over the straw; her feet are soaking wet."

"Is that all?"

"No, she's squatting down, with her legs apart. Her hands are on her knees."

"Has he come?"

"Not yet. She's bearing down, though, very hard. Wait a minute. I can see the top of his head sticking out. There's a lot of blood. She's pressing her belly with both hands. The whole head's out. He's alive."

"Are you sure?"

"He turned, by himself, to the left. She's grabbed hold of him, under the jaw, on either side. Here comes the left shoulder. The right one, too, and the arms. He's out. She pulled him out and put him down on the straw."

"Now what?"

"Just the afterbirth—it's all slimy—and more blood."

"Anything else?"

"Yes. She's picked him up again, by the heels."

"What about the cord?"

"She bit that off. Now she's tying it up."

"How?"

"With a piece of cloth from the hem of her dress; she tore it off."

"Tell me more."

"Not now," I said.

The afterbirth on the bloody straw buzzed with flies. Mrs. Tauber stood up with the baby in her arms. Then she reached beneath him, for the split seam, and ripped her dress from her left breast. It was swollen with milk; the veins stood out. She squeezed the nipple between her thumb and forefinger; a drop oozed from it.

Nikodomich said, "Nu?"

"He's got the teat in his mouth."

The log on the ground was still smoldering; the fire under the iron kettle had died down. She sang in a low voice,

Here, have a swig.
The rain has stopped.
The dove has gone
To build her nest
Between two sprigs of cedar
In the Lebanon . . .

I unbuttoned my fly and took out my prick. It got stiff and throbbed in my palm. The baby sucked away. She picked a wisp of straw from his head. His left hand tugged at the necklace between her breasts; the coins clinked together.

She raised her hand, his fist closed around her little finger, and she brought it up to her lips. Then she bit off his thumb, chewed it up, and swallowed it. Her mouth was smeared with blood. She stuck the second and third fingers between her teeth.

I stepped over Nikodomich, whose forehead was still pressed to the ground, and took off. The church looked deserted; the window was boarded up. On the Platz, in front of the Korpus, the Orenburg Cossack with blue stripes on his pants was feeding his horse an apple.

The downtown express roared overhead; the black horse pricked up its ears. I buttoned up my fly and ran across the street. The sidewalk was littered with husks from sunflower seeds, herring bones, and broken glass. Old man Isaacs was outside the Russian steam bath in his bare feet. He had his felt boots in one hand; in the other, a pair of brown calfskin shoes with high heels. The door behind him was slightly open, enough for me to sniff the steam. It smelled of eucalyptus leaves.

"What're you doing?" he asked me in English. "Are you crazy? Take off your shoes and socks. This is holy ground."

While balancing on one foot as I unlaced my right shoe, I woke up.

I went into the kitchen, without lighting the gas, and gulped down a handful of icy water from the tap. Then I sat on the stool.

From the doorway Mrs. Tauber said, "I thought I heard you roaming around. What's the trouble? Can't you sleep?"

She lit the gas jet on the wall above the icebox and turned it up. Her face was puffy; her bulging coat buttoned at the neck.

"What is it?" she asked. "Why are you crying?"

"I'm not crying."

She came over to me. "Yes, you are," she said. "Don't cry," and with her cold hands on my ears, she bent down and kissed the tear from the corner of my right eye.

ELMIRA, NEW YORK
1965